Darlene knew her plan was devious

Mac opened the door and stared at Darlene who was soaking wet from the heavy rainfall. She was panting and shivering at the same time and his pulse quickened. Lord! she was sexy. Then he remembered their argument. He couldn't allow himself to forget her deception.

"Darlene, what the—" His jaw quivered. She moved toward him and began to strip off her clothes. "I'll . . . uh, get a towel."

She took the towel. "I'm here to talk." She gazed around the room. "You know, a fire would be nice. And some brandy." Darlene tucked the towel around her, then raised her wineglass in a toast, "To a humdinger of a love affair. Mac Jackson, you're one helluva lover. The best I've ever known. It's been fun."

She stopped before him, and dropped the towel. "The real issue is . . . where do we go from here?"

From the moment sassy Darlene Clements began wading in the creek with Suzanna in *Hard to Resist*, author **Mary Tate Engels** couldn't wait to write Darlene's story. In *Loved by the Best*, when Mary had roving Darlene settle in the Smoky Mountains of Tennessee—where Mary spent much of her childhood—she knew Darlene had finally found home. And when Darlene met Mac Jackson, Mary knew these two special characters had found love. A true romantic, Mary loves writing and living in Tucson with her family.

Books by Mary Tate Engels

HARLEQUIN TEMPTATION

194–THE NESTING INSTINCT
215–SPEAK TO THE WIND
243–THE RIGHT TIME
267–BEST-LAID PLANS
295–RIPE FOR THE PICKING
351–HARD TO RESIST

Loved by the Best

MARY TATE ENGELS

Harlequin Books

TORONTO • NEW YORK • LONDON
AMSTERDAM • PARIS • SYDNEY • HAMBURG
STOCKHOLM • ATHENS • TOKYO • MILAN

Published October 1991

ISBN 0-373-25466-0

LOVED BY THE BEST

Printed in U.S.A.

1

"HEY THERE, SUGAR! A babe with a body that hot shouldn't hide it. Come on, give us a thrill!"

"You're such a tease. Show us more!"

"I could show you more," Darlene challenged with a smile as she placed her customers' drinks on the rough-hewn table. "But would you respect me in the morning?"

Two of the men chuckled and slapped their broad knees.

Another bearded bear of a man shouted, "It's respect ya want? I respect our right to know and your right to show!"

Every damn man in The Blue Boar looked like a giant, Darlene observed as she wove between the tables serving drinks. The bar was packed tonight with men who came from all over the country to take part in Gatlinburg's annual Highland Games. They were brawny—they had to be, Darlene supposed, to heave telephone poles and shots. And their groping aim wasn't bad, either—even after rounds and rounds of beer, which they swilled like there was no tomorrow. Well, she'd had *years* of practice at dodging paws and could deflect their roving hands with good-natured laughter.

"Honey, you're a sweetheart of a waitress—you're the best," a very drunk customer called out after Darlene slapped down another round on his table. She *was* one of the best, Darlene thought to herself as she walked off. Swift. Efficient. Tavern owners hired her on the spot. Customers took to her. At one time, she had taken pride in that. But now, as she approached her twenty-seventh birthday, she was beginning to wonder if that was something to be proud of...or if she had done *anything* she could point to with pride. Oh, she had produced a pretty fine kid. But she couldn't take full responsibility for him. She had her mother to thank for that. And her brother, Chase.

Waitressing held no challenge or interest anymore. It was just another job in yet another restaurant or bar. The crowds were all alike.

Worse yet, *Darlene* was still the same. Oh, she'd learned a thing or two and was a much better waitress now than when she started waitressing at sixteen. But she hadn't actually improved her lot in life over the years.

From the jukebox Willie Nelson whined, "Mommas, don't let your babies grow up to be cowboys." Darlene silently agreed.

She should have nixed her boyfriend's immature whim to go west. But she trusted Wiley and bought into his promises for more than four years. Oh, at first it had sounded exciting and fun. But years went by, and he couldn't land a job on any ranch in the whole of New Mexico, Arizona or Texas. They had tried them all, or so it seemed.

Finally, someone in the Texas panhandle had hired Wiley to drive a truckload of cotton back east. By then, they were so desperate for money, he'd been forced to take the job. Darlene had come along with him, although midway through the trip she'd wondered why. They had argued all the way across country, and by the time they reached the winding Tennessee mountain roads, they had settled into a stony silence.

During what was to be a brief stop in Gatlinburg, Tennessee, Darlene made her decision: She instructed Wiley to go on without her. With a shrug, Wiley had departed. Darlene had been amazed at how easily he left her after four years. Having no alternative then, she had pulled herself together and landed a job as a waitress at the local Blue Boar tavern.

Tonight, she couldn't say she was too thrilled with waitressing. As she made her way between the broad-shouldered men, Darlene put on a smile, trying to hide her feelings. She felt disappointed in herself. She was alone and lonely. Strange town. No friends. No family. She left her tray on the corner of the bar and gave another order to Stubbs Powell, the bartender and owner of The Blue Boar.

"How's it going tonight, Darlene?"

"They're drinking it down as fast as I can set 'em up." She placed her latest tab on the spindle.

"Great job! That's what you were hired to do." He glanced at her order and began opening bottles of beer.

"I told you I had experience and you wouldn't be sorry for hiring me."

He gave her a quick once-over. "You're lookin' real good in that blouse, sugar. Don't you want to show a little more cleavage? It would sure tickle the crowd tonight."

"That's *not* what I was hired for, Stubbs." Darlene's skimpy English-barmaid costume revealed more curves than she cared to. As tiny as she was, there was more of her than material. A black bodice cinched her waist and pushed her bosom up while a miniskirt barely came to the tops of her thighs. It was a degrading costume, but it went with the job.

"You could make more money," Stubbs suggested enticingly.

"From you or them?" She tossed her head, and the effort jiggled the little white cap perched on her blond hair.

"Both." Stubbs grinned and revealed a couple of spaces from missing teeth.

"The pay's not good enough."

"The pay will improve considerably, I promise you."

"I wasn't hired to strip."

"No, no. Just tease a little, like the barmaids in old England. Or Scotland. That's what these men are used to!" He winked and placed a double handful of longnecks on the tray. "Hey, pretend you're in another place, another time. Give us a little show."

"You've got the wrong barmaid, Stubbs," Darlene said smartly, snatching the tray and rattling the beer bottles as she made her way between the tables.

The night wore on and by one-thirty, Darlene was tired and glad to see the last of the customers leave. She helped clear the tables and wipe down the bar. While Stubbs was still counting the cash, she reached into the bottom drawer of the cabinet for her purse.

"Good night, Stubbs. Thanks for the job." She hoped to slip out without any more contact with her boss. There was something about him that she didn't trust.

"You were pretty good tonight, Darlene. I think you're going to work out fine for The Boar. You catch on quick."

She hoped he caught on that she was here to wait tables, *and that was all.* A part of her was indeed grateful for the job. Another part of her hated it. "See you tomorrow."

"No, not tomorrow. Don't forget, we're closed Sunday and Monday. You're scheduled to work next Tuesday night. Can I count on you to be here?"

"Oh, yes." She started toward the door, glad to have a couple of days off before the whole miserable routine started again.

But suddenly Stubbs was beside her, circling her wrist with his huge mitt of a hand. Darlene felt uneasy, and she squirmed out of his grasp. "Maybe you'll be a little more friendly to the customers next time, huh, Darlene?"

"What do you mean by that?" She lifted her chin defiantly. "I thought I did okay."

"You did just fine." He stepped in front of her, blocking her way to the door. "But you could do better. You know—" he gestured "—maybe you could loosen that ribbon a little."

Instinctively her free hand went to the thin black ribbon that gathered her blouse at the front. She jerked her other hand from his grip, reacting angrily to his implication. "I told you before. I wasn't hired for that."

His voice lowered. "You could make two hundred a night, sugar. Plus tips. Now, who can turn down two hundred or more a night? Can you, Darlene?"

She looked up at him. She *could* use the money to help her get back home. Who couldn't use a thousand a week? For a woman in her shoes, it was a tempting proposition. But she resisted. She'd have to give up too much. Her dignity was about all she had left at this point. She narrowed her eyes. "No way, Stubbs."

"Come on, sugar, why don't you give me a little sneak preview?" He ran his thick fingers lightly along the top of one breast.

Darlene shivered at his touch. She jumped backward, causing Stubbs's fat fingers to rake down hard, ripping the front of her blouse. Immediately she knew she was in trouble; and too late, she wondered if any of the cleanup crew were still in the back room. She hadn't heard anyone in the last few minutes. "Get away from me, Stubbs." She backed up, stalling for time, trying to figure out how she could get past him.

He chuckled. "The boys have all gone home. It's jus' you 'n' me."

Darlene's heart pounded with cold fear. She could smell whiskey on his breath. He had been drinking, and she hadn't even noticed it. Lord, she must be slipping. She had been so preoccupied with her own problems tonight that she hadn't detected such an important detail. She could usually sense danger, especially from a boss. But this one had surprised her. And it was her own damn fault.

Darlene dodged his groping arms and made an effort to get past him and run out the door. Stubbs lunged frantically for her. One broad, outstretched palm caught her cheek, hard. The impact made a loud smacking sound. Darlene gasped at the stinging pain. She was hurt—and furious.

As their bodies brushed, Darlene drew her knee up sharply into his groin. His agonizing groan told her she had hit her target and bought herself a little time.

While Stubbs was bent forward, moaning and cursing, Darlene scrambled for the door. She dropped her purse, but now was not the time to hesitate, so she left it. She had to get away from him.

Outside the bar's back door was a small, raised porch with a steep stairway that led down to the alley. Darlene practically leaped for those stairs, just as a noise at the door indicated that Stubbs was right behind her. In her frantic attempt to escape, she tripped, lost her balance and fell over the railing. She landed hard behind a cluster of garbage cans.

The back door opened and Stubbs stood there, heaving and muttering low curses. The night was dead quiet. Darlene lay very still, feeling pain but not daring to move. If Stubbs found her, there'd be another battle. And next time, she might not be so lucky. She couldn't risk it.

With a barrage of curses, Stubbs slammed the door shut. Darlene let her breath out carefully. She would get up as soon as it was safe—and she was able.

THE SUDDEN ACTIVITY and the clattering noises from the garbage cans caught the attention of a young couple parked in the alley.

"Someone fell from those steps, Danny."

"Hmm? You sure?"

"I think somebody fell into those trash cans. Didn't you hear the cans rattle?"

Danny glanced at the clock on the dashboard, then groaned. "Oh, Lord! Look what time it is! Your pa's going to kill me, Kayrn. It's nearly two."

"What do you think he'll do to *me?* I'll be grounded till I'm twenty!" She clutched his hand. "Listen, Danny, I swear I hear something. Let's go see who fell off the stairs."

"Maybe we shouldn't get involved."

"Maybe somebody's hurt over there."

"Okay, but we have to be very careful," Danny said.

Cautiously, Danny and Kayrn crept toward the garbage cans.

"Look, Danny! It's a woman. Omigosh, she's hurt!"

Darlene didn't move. Her mind instructed her to get up, but her body refused to obey. She kept her eyes closed, hoping these two people would go away.

"We'd better call the police about this, Kayrn."

"No, you don't! My pa would find out we were here for sure, then."

"What'll we do? Leave her here?"

"We can't do that. Why don't we take her to some public place where she'll be noticed?"

"Like where?"

"How about the church steps? Reverend Beatty would see that she was taken care of."

"Naw, Kayrn. Lookit the way she's dressed. She came from that bar upstairs. The Blue Boar."

"How about leaving her at the hospital door?"

"Somebody might recognize my car and tell your pa it was us that brought her in."

"Well, we can't leave her here, Danny. She might die. She might already be dead."

"I'd better check." Danny knelt down beside Darlene. When Darlene sat up and glared at him, he jumped back about a foot.

"I'm not dead," Darlene declared. "So cool it! But my head sure hurts."

"Thank goodness," Kayrn murmured, then added apologetically, "Uh, not that your head hurts, ma'am, but that you're all right."

Darlene touched various parts of her body. "Seems to be all here. Just get me out of this trash."

Danny took one arm and clumsily helped her to her feet. "You sure you're all right, ma'am?"

Darlene nodded sullenly. "I think so." But she was beginning to have doubts as she felt her body start to throb with pain.

"Can we take you home?"

"Yeah, that'd be nice. I just live down the street." She hesitated, recalling that Stubbs was the one who'd found the apartment for her. If he really wanted to aggravate her further, he knew exactly where to find her. "No, maybe that's not such a hot idea. It may not be safe."

"You mean safe from whoever was chasing you down the stairs?" Kayrn asked.

Darlene hugged her bare arms, nervously rubbing one of them. "He. . . he knows where to find me, if he wants to. I don't know what to do."

"I know a safe place," Danny offered. "Mac takes care of my injured animals all the time. He won't mind."

Darlene shook her head. "You don't have to bother anyone. I can take care of myself. I'll find something."

"Please," Kayrn urged. "I'd feel better if you were with Mac."

Darlene gazed from one to the other. "I don't even know you. Worse yet, you don't know me. And who the heck is Mac?"

"I'm Kayrn Grider. And this is Danny Blalock. His folks run Blalock's Motel and Restaurant downtown."

Darlene smiled gratefully at them. They seemed sincere in wanting to help her. So why not let them? "I'm Darlene Clements, and I'm new in town. This was my first night on the job. And my last," she added bitterly. "But that's not your concern. Thanks for checking on me, but there's no need for you to get more involved. I can take care of myself."

"Maybe so," Kayrn replied. "But what if this guy tries to find you and . . . ?"

"Oh, I, uh—" Darlene stopped and shrugged. She didn't know what would happen. It wasn't something she wanted to consider.

"That does it," Kayrn decided. She took Darlene by the arm and started toward the car. "Mac'll know exactly what to do."

"Who's this Mac?" Darlene asked as she climbed obediently into the back seat.

"He's someone you can trust," Danny said with conviction as he started the car.

Darlene sat quietly for a moment as they pulled away. Suddenly her long-denied mothering instincts were aroused. "Isn't it pretty late for you two to be out? I think you'd better take Kayrn home, Danny."

"Yes, ma'am," he agreed solemnly. "I'll take her home first since Mac lives out of town a ways."

Darlene rested her head on the seat back, trying to gather her wits and wondering about this person named Mac whom these kids seemed to trust completely.

MAC JACKSON WAS sound asleep when the howling bark of his floppy-eared hound woke him. Headlights lit his driveway and aimed for the house. He threw the cover off his lean, naked body and glanced at the digital clock. Two-thirty. Who in the world could that be at this hour?

Sliding into a pair of worn jeans, he peered out the window. He recognized Danny Blalock sprinting toward the porch. Mac grabbed a T-shirt and pulled it over his head as he hurried through the house.

"Hush, Ace," Mac admonished the dog as he swung open the front door. "Danny, what are you doing here? Are you all right?"

"Yes, sir. Sorry to bother you so late." Danny motioned for Mac to follow him to the car. "But I'm in a squeeze!"

"Is it your dad?" Without pausing or bothering to get shoes, Mac went with the boy.

"No, it's cool unless he catches me out this late. Honestly, Mac, I wouldn't have come here tonight except I didn't know who else to tell. We figured you'd know what to do about this."

"Not another injured animal, Danny—"

"No, sir," he vowed in his rich Southern accent. He opened the car's back door. "She's a woman."

Mac's eyes took a moment to focus in the partial darkness. The figure in the back seat was small, scantily clad, with big eyes and long legs, and, in the muted light, looked gorgeous. He whistled under his breath. "She sure is, Danny."

The young woman lifted her head and gazed at him with captivating dark eyes. For a moment she reminded him of a trapped animal. Then he saw her more clearly, and he thought of a cheetah, wild and exotically beautiful and, not by any stretch of the imagination, trapped. He could see tremendous pride and determination in those deep brown eyes of hers.

"I know it must look bad, Mac," Danny continued in a rush. "But it's not what you think. She tripped on The Blue Boar's back stairs. You know the high ones in the alley? Kayrn'll vouch for me."

"I'll bet," Mac replied.

"Kayrn and I happened to, uh, find her."

Mac scoffed. "You *happened* to be in the alley behind The Blue Boar at two in the morning? C'mon, Danny."

"It was only one forty-five then. And I've already taken her home. We didn't *do* anything, Mac. We, uh, fell asleep."

"That is the oldest excuse in the book," Mac muttered sarcastically and motioned toward the woman. "So you found her in the alley and brought her here?" He stepped back and turned his head to Danny and whispered, "Why, for God's sake?"

"We didn't know what to do with her and thought she might be hurt. Anyway, she was afraid to go home because someone was after her."

Darlene had heard enough. "I am *not* scared, just cautious. All I need is a place to spend the rest of the night. Danny said you'd help me. Said you could be trusted."

"Well, I'd like to think that," Mac drawled. "But who are you running from? What happened?"

Her brown eyes flashed defiantly. "My boss at The Blue Boar got a little rambunctious, and when I tried to get away, I tripped on the stairs and fell behind the garbage cans. I guess it must have scared Danny and Kayrn. They thought I was hurt bad. But I'm not. Look, I won't cause you any trouble, mister. And tomorrow, I'll leave."

Mac narrowed his gaze when he took in the red welt on her cheek. "Stubbs is after you? Did he hit you?"

"No, I didn't say that. I just took a fall." She eyed him steadily. It wasn't quite a lie, yet not the whole truth, either. She had the uncomfortable feeling that this man with the piercing eyes could see through her, even in the dark. "I'm all right. Honest."

Mac stuffed his hands in his back pockets and evaluated the woman. She looked okay, except for the red mark on her cheek that promised to become a shiner by tomorrow. Had Stubbs hit her? Or had she damaged herself when she fell, as she claimed?

"Well, can I stay or not?" Darlene gestured impatiently. "Danny's got to go home. It's late."

Mac shrugged. "I guess so." He couldn't help wondering if she was drunk—and if agreeing to this wasn't a big mistake.

Of all the offbeat things that had happened to him, this was the strangest. A beautiful, scantily clad woman appears out of the blue at two-thirty in the morning, and she claims she only wants to spend the night. He must be dreaming! And crazy, to boot! He watched her climb out of the car.

Her legs were slender and sleek in black fishnet stockings. A skimpy costume barely covered her slim body and revealed enough to make a man's imagination go wild. She kept one hand modestly at her bosom—to hide, he suspected, her exposed cleavage. Then he saw the torn blouse. His suspicions were confirmed. More had happened to her than Danny had seen—and more than she was telling.

"I, uh, Kayrn and I hoped you wouldn't tell our folks, Mac," Danny said in a worried tone. "We didn't intend to stay so late. It just *happened*. I swear. We were just parked there and—"

"You know I won't snitch on you, Danny. But we *will* discuss this later. What you did was dangerous, in more ways than one. Go on home now." Mac waved his hand to dismiss him and reached out to help the woman, who seemed to be somewhat unsteady on her feet.

"It's all true. You can ask Kayrn." The boy began sidestepping toward the driver's side. "I gotta go, before my old man realizes I'm gone. Talk to you tomorrow, Mac. And, thanks."

As the car pulled out of sight, Mac and Darlene made their way toward his house, a log-and-stone structure nestled in the pines. He hobbled barefoot over the gravel. She teetered in her spike-heeled shoes. They mounted the steps to an old-fashioned, rail-lined porch, and Mac mumbled something to the floppy-eared hound that blocked the doorway. The dog shuffled aside, and Mac switched on the light.

Darlene blinked and curiously looked around the living room. There was a small desk in the corner holding a typewriter and a lamp. A sheet of white paper dangled from the typewriter's carriage, rippling in the occasional breeze from an open window next to the desk.

On the other side of the room, a cushioned chair and sofa sat at right angles. The sofa was piled high with pillows and looked invitingly comfortable. Then Darlene's gaze settled on Mac, the man she was supposed to trust for the rest of the night.

He was tall and broad-shouldered with slightly-longer-than-stylish brown hair and a short, dark beard that emphasized his square jaw. His face was angular, and he looked hungry or angry—certainly less than satisfied with life. Most unique about this large man, though, were his stunningly blue eyes. They seemed to assess her, strip her, and yet treat her with kindness, all at the same time.

She clutched her torn blouse together to hide her breasts and nodded toward the three-seater sofa. "I'll be glad to sleep there. Just toss me a blanket."

"Wouldn't you rather sleep in the spare bedroom?" he questioned, watching her closely. "In a real bed? With sheets?" Mac figured that she had been in some sort of a scuffle. Even in the low lighting, he could see that the abrasion on the fragile skin covering her cheekbone was turning into an ugly bruise.

"Well, yes." She smiled faintly, and he detected a bit of light in her tired, brown eyes.

"I'll admit I'm curious about you," he said in a slow drawl. "Like your, ah, name."

"I'm Darlene Clements."

"Nice to meet you, Darlene. I'm McLane Jackson. Everyone calls me Mac. And this—" he indicated the long-eared dog "—is Ace. He doesn't quite come up to the name, but I keep hoping. Are you from around here?"

Darlene shook her head. "No, I—" She started to say she was just passing through, but somehow she knew that wouldn't sound as stable as "I'm new here. And I'm really bushed."

"I'll bet. It's been quite a night, huh?"

Darlene propped one fist on her hip and mocked his drawl with one of her own. "Look, Mac, you don't have to worry about me ruining your reputation by sleeping over. I'll be gone first thing in the morning. No one will ever know I was here. Those kids don't want anyone to know they found me at that hour, so they won't squeal. Stubbs Powell certainly doesn't want his actions known. And no one else in town knows me at all."

"What did Stubbs do to you?" Mac sat on the broad, cushioned chair arm, hoping by his relaxed attitude to lower her defenses. He dropped his hands casually between his thighs as he straddled the chair. "I couldn't help noticing that your blouse is torn. And you've got that hickey under your eye. Did he rape you?"

"No, of course not!" Her answer was quick and definite. Her dark eyes flashed angrily. "He was drunk. He pawed me a little. I don't think he was capable of rape."

"Don't underestimate the man."

She stuck her chin out. "Don't underestimate *me*. I was in control, not him."

"Then don't make excuses for his violence." Mac was sure, now, that the bruise on her cheek hadn't come from her falling over the stair railing. She was a little too defensive.

"I'm not making excuses..." Darlene faltered, knowing that she probably wasn't even thinking straight tonight. "Look, I'm very tired. Could we discuss this tomorrow? I can deal with your questions much better after a few hours' sleep."

"I thought you were leaving first thing in the morning."

"Then I'll send you a letter, explaining everything in full," she snapped.

Realizing he was getting nowhere, Mac stood and shrugged. "Okay, Darlene. We'll talk tomorrow. I have to get up very early in the morning. In a couple of hours, in fact. But I should be back around noon. You get some rest, and we'll talk then." He motioned as he started down the hall.

She followed his T-shirt-and-jeans-clad figure. His feet were bare, and the fact seemed strangely sensual. Darlene sensed that he was naked under those snug-fitting jeans; *that* thought was downright provocative. She cleared her throat and tried to think of something else. "You have to get up in a couple of hours? What in the world for?"

"To take some tourists fishing and help them catch trout from the mountain streams. It's not as easy as it seems. You know, it's amazing what people will pay for when they're on vacation."

"My brother does that, only it's a different kind and method of fishing. He runs a little fishing village in the Bull Shoals area of Arkansas. Mostly they fish for bass from boats that they rent from him."

"Is that where you're from? Arkansas?"

"Uh-hmm. A long time ago."

Mac tucked the information away and reached inside one dark doorway to flip on the light as they passed. "Bathroom," he announced unceremoniously and went on to the next door. "Bedroom. Make yourself at home."

Darlene walked into the room and looked around. *Home?* she reflected ironically. It was as good as any she'd had. Better than most. The furnishings were simple, and the place was clean. She smiled faintly at Mac. Was she assuming too much by trusting him? He looked honest enough, but who could tell by looks these days? "This'll be fine, thanks."

It was probably a risk, taking a bed in this strange man's house, considering she had only the recommendation of a couple of kids she'd never met before tonight. But the man had honest eyes. That wasn't much, she realized. Lately her instincts hadn't been working very well. First Wiley, then Stubbs.

Right now, though, she had no choice but to trust Mac Jackson. His house definitely seemed safer than the little flat she'd rented down the street from The Blue

Boar. And she really couldn't trust Stubbs not to break into it in the middle of the night.

"There're a few old clothes in some of the drawers," he said, gesturing to the dresser. "Help yourself to a T-shirt and jeans."

"Thanks," she murmured, glancing in the mirror. The reflection gazing back at her looked almost like a stranger's. Her torn costume was like something out of the sixteenth century. Her eyes were red-rimmed and tired. Her full lips quivered slightly, as if she were on the verge of tears. Her disheveled blond hair was missing the perky little barmaid's hat. The oval face with the too-big eyes reflected a little girl lost, but the pouting lips tightened to reveal a tough-as-nails woman who could conquer anything.

Darlene narrowed her eyes and pressed her lips together firmly. She had no time or patience for self-pity or tears. She needed to get some rest, so she could go about finding herself a decent job tomorrow. She'd already decided she wouldn't be working for Stubbs Powell anymore.

"Do you need anything else?"

"No, thank you, Mac. This'll be fine."

"Good night, Darlene," Mac said, retreating into the hall. "Sleep well."

"Oh, uh, Mac?" She turned to him.

He gazed at her steadily, his blue eyes assessing all of her.

"Thanks for, uh, taking me in. I know this is a big inconvenience, especially since you have to get up so soon. But I appreciate it."

He nodded matter-of-factly. "No problem, Darlene. G'night."

With a little smile on her strained face, Darlene closed the door. She couldn't help liking him, warming to the way he said her name—*Drr-leen*—sliding it all together into one syllable. She felt that she could trust Mac—at least, she hoped so. She locked the door, just in case.

2

CHURCH BELLS WOKE Darlene at noon. She forced herself to get up. She vaguely remembered being brought to a stranger's house last night. More vivid was the recollection that the bearded stranger had the kindest blue eyes she'd ever seen.

Darlene struggled to her feet. The way her body ached and her head throbbed reminded her of the time she'd ridden a bronc on a bet with Wiley. Oh, how she had so stupidly entertained him! She'd lost the bet, and even though nothing had been broken, it had taken her a week to recover from the fall.

She moved clumsily, painfully, across the room and glanced in the dresser mirror. The sight of her reflection halted—and angered—her. She glared at the smudgy bruise on her cheek. The area under her eye was starting to discolor. She'd have a shiner by nighttime.

"Dammit! How the heck can I get a new job looking like a prizefighter? Oh, Lord, I'm ruined!" Disgusted with her appearance, she turned away from the mirror. What a mess she'd gotten herself into!

She opened the door and stepped into the hall. "What are you staring at?" she snapped at the floppy-eared hound who watched her with sad, solemn eyes. Her own eyes, she knew, looked the same. And that made her even angrier.

Darlene was alone with the dog, and the house was ominously quiet. She went into the bathroom and turned on the light. She knew what she had to do—shower, then get the heck out of here.

SHORTLY AFTER one o'clock in the afternoon, Mac turned his Jeep Cherokee onto Bear Creek Road. He propped his elbow in the open window and pressed the accelerator, taking little notice of the lush green-carpeted fields dotted with hickory trees on either side. Tall oaks spread their thick-leaved branches to shade the few horses that grazed here and there. A small stream threaded its way beside the road, seeking the larger Bear Creek.

Mac had lived here most of his life. After those few miserable years in Kentucky, he had returned to the mountains that he loved.

The mountains had provided a haven when he needed it, and if the truth be known, they remained a place to escape the world of big business that he now despised. But it wasn't the past or the mountains that Mac was thinking of today. It was the attractive woman who'd appeared on his doorstep and who'd been asleep in his spare room when he left this morning.

He wondered if she'd still be there now. Mac figured Darlene would sleep until noon or so, then she'd probably take a shower, eat a bite and . . . leave. Of course, that's what she'd do. She wouldn't hang around waiting for him, even though he'd left her a note saying he would be back in the early afternoon and would take her home then. No. If she was as headstrong as she seemed to be last night, Darlene would probably strike out on her own.

Mac rounded a curve and, not surprisingly, spotted her hitchhiking in the opposite direction to where he was headed. She looked ridiculous dressed in his clothes, but even that wasn't surprising to him. What else was she to wear? That skimpy costume she'd arrived in last night? Hardly.

His large T-shirt hung loosely on her slender body and was gathered into a knot at her hip. His bulky jeans were cinched at her tiny waist with one of his belts. Her spike heels were the ones that went with black fishnet stockings to make her legs look like a million bucks. Her hair sparkled like gold in the sunlight, and she appeared glamorous and comical at the same time.

Mac pulled alongside her and stopped. "Hi. Going somewhere?"

She propped one hand on her hip and retorted snidely, "No, I'm just out walking for my health."

"Want a ride?"

"No, thanks. I'm going the other way, back to town."

"You've got quite a nice walk ahead, then. It's seven miles from here."

"I'll catch a ride."

He glanced doubtfully down the empty road. "You planning on taking off in my clothes?"

"I intend to return them as soon as I can."

"Oh?" He looked back at her. At this moment, she could be in an ad for expensive jeans—one of those low-key, black-and-white photo sessions that show various shots of a denim-clad beauty in some remote location, like the Smoky Mountains. "How do you expect to do that?"

She tossed her head. "I'll figure out a way."

"Uh-hmm. I'll bet."

"I will!" she insisted. "I'm going to get another job and— Anyway, why would I want to keep these old things?" She made a sweeping gesture from shoulder to thigh.

His gaze followed the graceful motion of her hand. "You're right. They don't do a thing for you. Come on, and I'll take you—"

"No, thanks. I'm heading back to town."

"Dar-lene," he said with a deliberate pause, dragging her name into two long syllables. "In case you haven't noticed by now, this road isn't highly traveled. Your chances of catching a ride to town are slim or none. Get in, and I'll take you where you need to go."

"Mac, I've imposed on you enough. I'll find my own way. I'm used to fending for myself. There comes a car now. See?" She stuck her thumb out for the vehicle that slowed to thread between where she stood on the side of the narrow, two-lane road and the opposite lane, where Mac had halted his Jeep. The car made no effort to stop for her, though.

She glared at it as it sped away.

"What's wrong with you?" Mac yelled at her, angry now that he saw she really intended to hitch a ride. "You can't ride with perfect strangers! It isn't safe."

"What do you think *you* are?" she countered. "And I spent the entire night with you!"

"Yes, but you knew— Oh, never mind! Just get in."

She turned a defiant gaze on him. Without saying a word, she refused.

He opened the door and placed one foot on the pavement. Leaning his elbow on the sill of the open window, he bent toward her. "Let me explain something, Darlene. The only people traveling on this road are families who live around here and know each other well, or tourists renting cabins down by the creek. Neither are about to stop and pick up a strange woman dressed in men's clothes and carrying a knapsack, looking like she's running away from home."

She shook the plastic bag she carried. "My stupid costume! It goes back to Stubbs—in his nose!"

"You look like a hobo!"

"You don't look much better!" she shot back.

"I've been fishing!" He ran his hand down the front of his camouflage shirt and gestured toward the passenger seat with his thumb. "Get in this Jeep!"

She scowled at him for a minute, then sighing with frustration, stomped around the vehicle. "All right! All right, you win!" Her voice was shrill and loud. She made an effort to lower it an octave by the time she crawled into the seat beside him. "Here I am. Are you satisfied? Now, take me home, please."

He nodded and continued traveling in the direction of his house.

"I told you, I'm not going this way!" she insisted.

"But *I* am. And you're with me."

"Unfortunately."

"Is this the way you show gratitude?"

She shot a dagger gaze at him. "Don't try anything with me. After last night, I won't hesitate to—"

"Hey, cool down. I'm only interested in taking a quick shower." He glared at her. "Nothing more."

She shifted slightly and took a breath. "Okay."

He drove with one large hand on the steering wheel, the other on the gearshift between them. She sat stiffly, looking straight ahead. He'd never seen anyone so uppity—especially when she had so little to be uppity about. Why, she didn't even own the shirt on her back. "I didn't get much sleep last night, and a shower will give me a little refresher," he said, making a stab at casual conversation.

"If you want gratitude, thank you very much," she responded tightly. "If you want an apology, forget it. I told you I didn't want to impose on you any more than I already have. You can let me out of here anytime."

"You stay right where you are."

"You know something, Mac Jackson?" She glared at him with narrowed eyes. "You are one damned stubborn man."

"You, Darlene Clements, are one to talk." He shook his head and chuckled. "It's like the pot calling the kettle black. I've never seen such a damned stubborn woman."

"I guess that makes us a pair."

After a pause, he corrected slowly, "No, it doesn't make us anything."

She clamped her lips together and gazed out the window, convinced that he was an absolute jerk. They rounded another curve in stony silence.

A woman standing on the front porch of a house near the road waved at the Jeep. Mac returned the wave and drew to a halt. "Ida's my neighbor," he told Darlene before calling, "Howdy, Ida! How's everything?"

"Fine as frog's hair," she called back to him. "Why don't you come on over for Sunday dinner? I have enough for an army."

"Can't." He gestured toward Darlene with his head. "Company."

"Bring her along! Boyd wanted to talk to you about something important, anyway." She smiled. "I made fried chicken, Mac. And mashed potatoes and gravy. And cherry pie!"

"Sounds great, Ida." Mac looked at Darlene. "How about it? Does the best Southern-fried chicken you've ever had sound good? Ida's cherry pie takes the prize at the fair every year."

Darlene shrugged, not wanting to admit it, but she hadn't had a decent meal since the day Wiley left her in Gatlinburg. She hadn't dared spend the little bit of money in her purse. Which was still in The Blue Boar where she'd dropped it last night. She couldn't eat until she got it back. "I . . ."

"I'm starved," Mac encouraged with a half grin. "Sounds good to me."

Just the thought of food made Darlene's stomach growl. "You sure they won't mind?"

"Not a bit. They'll be offended now, if we don't go."

She only hesitated another moment. "Well, okay."

He grinned, then called to Ida, "We'll be over soon!" The Jeep rolled forward again and he commented, "You won't be sorry. Ida's a great cook. And afterward, I'll take you home."

"It's nice of her to invite us."

"Typical. Ida's a fine woman. I sometimes wonder how such a nice lady could have such a jerk for a son."

"Boyd?"

"Yep."

"What's wrong with him?"

"Irresponsible, arrogant and narrow-minded."

Darlene laughed. "Sounds like most men to me."

"Well, you're wrong."

"Oh?" She angled her head and gave him a challenging look. "*You're* different?"

"Yep."

She shook her head and scoffed, "I doubt it." When he didn't defend his position, she continued: "I sure could use a cigarette right now. I couldn't find any at your house, Mac. Do you smoke?"

"Nope." He turned into his driveway.

"You don't have any stuffed away somewhere that somebody left?"

"None."

"What about your neighbors?" The thought of *not* having a cigarette made her *want* one even more.

"Ida?" He shook his head and switched off the engine. "No way. And Boyd quit a year ago. Smartest thing he ever did."

She sighed and it came out as a low groan. "Then I have to go all afternoon without a cigarette?"

"Guess so." Mac slammed the driver's door and began hauling fishing equipment out of the back of the Jeep.

Darlene slid out of the Jeep and grabbed a couple of items before following him around to the back of the house. She needed a cigarette badly. But how the heck could she get one where there were none to be found? She was seven miles from town and the nearest store. Great.

Mac stashed his load on a shelf in the garage and turned to take what she had carried. His rough hand brushed hers as he took the wicker creel for storing fish and the fishing rod. Her touch was electric, and he felt the physical attraction even as they continued to spar. "This might be a good time to stop smoking, since you'll be without a cigarette for so long."

She swiftly countered him. "No, this is *not* a good time to stop smoking. And I don't plan to be without one any longer than necessary." Furious at the notion, she followed him to the back door. Just as they stepped inside, the phone rang.

Darlene pretended not to listen, but couldn't help herself when she heard her name and realized the conversation was about her.

"Hi, Danny," Mac was saying. "No, no, don't worry. It's all right. She's fine. Has a pretty bad bruise on her cheek and it looks like it'll turn into a black eye, but she'll be okay in a day or two." Mac paused. "You did exactly the right thing." There was another pause, then a little chuckle. "Yes, we both have a secret. We'll discuss this later."

He hung up and looked at Darlene. "That was Danny asking about your welfare. You do remember Danny, don't you?"

"Of course," Darlene huffed. "He's the boy who brought me here."

"He was worried about you."

"I figured he was more worried that one of us would tell his dad that he and Kayrn were parked in that alley."

"That's a pretty good guess."

She looked up curiously. "You won't tell, will you, Mac?"

"No. But I plan to have a few words with him about the dangers of stolen love in a parked car."

She laughed wryly. "I could give him some firsthand advice about that."

Mac tucked away another bit of information about Darlene. "Basically Danny's a good kid, although he's battling hormones like every other seventeen-year-old. Wants to be a veterinarian. He often brings me wounded animals that he finds and leaves them out here while he nurses them back to health. He lives in town, and his parents won't allow animals there. I thought he was bringing me another wounded critter last night when he arrived with you."

"Surprise, surprise," Darlene drawled. She stuffed her hands in the jeans pockets, and the motion drew them tightly against her slim hips. "It's not causing a social problem for you to have a woman spend the night, is it?"

His blue eyes flickered, and she suspected he wasn't telling her the whole truth. "Not at all. Anyway, Danny'll keep it quiet."

"What about Ida? I'm sure she'll figure it out, if she hasn't already."

"She's no problem. Tends to her own affairs." He headed through the living room. "What kind of job are you looking for, Darlene?"

She followed him. "I don't know. Anything except being a waitress. I just want something temporary. I don't intend to stay here for long."

He nodded. "Not a waitress, huh? What other skills do you have? Typing?"

"No. But I can do other things."

"Like?"

She shrugged. "Anything. I can do anything I set my mind to."

He gazed at her questioningly, waiting for more.

"Trouble is," she continued, "who's going to hire someone with a black eye? Maybe I could get one of those jobs calling people, trying to sell pure water systems or solar hot-water panels."

Her smile was momentarily lighthearted and revealed yet another side of her. It was a side she kept well hidden, but one he couldn't resist wanting to know.

"Might be tough finding something like that in Gatlinburg. Almost everything is tourist related," he explained. "Today's Highland Games are a big event. Brings in lots of tourists. You just missed the Ramp Festival, but you're in time for the Run Fer Th' Hills Footrace."

She wrinkled her nose. "What's a ramp?"

"Like an onion, only worse." He shook his head. "Much worse."

She shrugged and ambled around the room. "I'll worry about a job tomorrow."

"Sounds like another famous Southern lady," he said with a grin. "A fictional one."

"You mean Scarlett O'Hara?" Darlene squared her shoulders. "She did pretty fine for herself, didn't she?"

"Yes, but this is a different era. You need skills." He motioned toward the typewriter on the desk. "Use my typewriter to practice if you'd like. That may be your best bet for a job around here."

"I don't . . . know how to type."

He gazed at her with a frown. "At the risk of sounding sexist, you should know typing. Everyone should be able to type—men as well as women. It's a valuable skill to have, especially in the age of computers."

Darlene stared skeptically at the little machine. Typing wasn't her idea of a valuable skill, but here she was with *no* skills. "I wouldn't know where to start."

Mac flipped a switch, and the typewriter made a low purr. "It's electric, so it's quick and easy. Here—" he inserted a clean sheet of paper "—play around with it. Write a letter. Or just get the feel of it. I'll show you some basics later. It isn't difficult to learn." He disappeared into the bathroom.

Soon Darlene could hear the water running for his shower. She imagined Mac's lean body standing naked under the spray—broad, angular shoulders, tapering to a narrow waist and slim hips. . . . Was his body hairy or sleek, and—? She shuddered and turned her attention to the typewriter, which hummed softly as if enticing her to hit the first key. She pressed the *d* and before she could lift her finger, the machine whirred and made a line of *d*'s across the page. "Quick and easy," Mac had said. And he was right.

Darlene pulled up the chair and began pecking at the typewriter one letter at a time, with no sense or order to her operation. She played with it, hitting a key, checking to see what it looked like, and hitting another. It was like magic to push a button and make a clearly legible black letter appear on the white page. She thought about writing something to Ken. Wouldn't he love to receive a letter from his mother?

A rush of enthusiasm spurred her to quickly remove the paper covered with her randomly chosen characters and insert a clean sheet. With effort, she managed to type, Dearrr kKKen.

She looked at her work. Not great, but readable. Wouldn't Ken be surprised to hear from her? The message was short. She told him that she was okay and visiting the Smoky Mountains. It wasn't the *whole* truth, but nearly. The countryside reminded her a little of home in the Ozarks, she said, and she wanted to come back and see him soon. That was definitely the truth. She couldn't help smiling with satisfaction as she rolled the paper out of the typewriter.

By the time Mac had finished his shower and opened the bathroom door, Darlene had folded the letter and tucked it safely into her bra.

In a few minutes Mac joined her. His wet brown hair, combed sleek against his head, had taken on a dark, rich mahogany hue. His clean, sweet-woods fragrance assaulted her senses and reminded her that he was extremely appealing. His beard, though short and neatly trimmed, gave his features a rough-hewn, textured look, and made him seem right at home here in the mountains. Otherwise, his face had a straight-nosed pleasantness that would fit anywhere.

He wore his soft blue T-shirt and faded, well-worn jeans that hugged his hips with a natural ease. He was barefoot—a detail that she remembered about his appearance last night. Those exposed, unprotected feet were somehow very sensual to her. His arms were sinewy and muscular—obviously strong. Prominent veins trailed from where his shirt sleeves were rolled to the elbows, down to his large, tanned hands.

Darlene especially liked his eyes—blue and sometimes piercing, sometimes angry. He'd certainly been angry at her often enough over the past twelve hours. But, even though they argued a lot, she liked him—sort of.

"Ida will ask questions about you," he bluntly informed her as he sat on the edge of the chair and began putting on his shoes and socks. "We need to figure out what you want her to know at this point."

"I have nothing to hide," Darlene said defiantly.

"Good. Then you don't mind if she knows you were working at The Blue Boar?"

"Well, I only worked there one night," Darlene hedged. "I'll just skip that part."

"Then, what are you doing here?"

"Visiting," she answered firmly.

"Visiting who?"

"Why, you, of course." She grinned, and flickers of devilment danced in her brown eyes. "Tell her we're cousins."

"Cousins?" He stiffened, and his blue eyes cut into her.

"Distant, of course."

"I thought you had nothing to hide."

She shrugged. "This sounds better."

"Do you have family in Arkansas?" he asked with a sudden intensity in his tone. "Real family?"

Darlene blinked at him and after a moment, nodded. "My brother, Chase, and his family still live there."

"No one else?" Mac was wondering about a boyfriend, or possibly a husband. *Oh, God! What if she has a husband somewhere . . . looking for her?*

Darlene was thinking of her son, and she didn't easily share that information, so she said, "Mama died years ago, and Pa left us too long ago to remember. There were just the two of us—Chase and me."

"And you came here looking for work?" Mac questioned doubtfully.

"Yep." She folded her arms. "Haven't you ever known a woman who was on her own before? A woman doesn't *have* to have a man to follow around all the time."

Mac nodded slowly. She was a little too defensive to be convincing. "Oh, yes. I've known my share of independent women. But something tells me you aren't really here by choice."

"I'm not in this shape by choice!" She took a seat on the sofa and slumped back. "What difference does it make, anyway?"

He shrugged. "It doesn't matter to me." Even as he said it, Mac knew it was a lie. He cared. But he couldn't pinpoint why, other than the fact that he'd never known a woman quite like this one. She was tough and tenacious. And she had miles of spunk. Maybe that's what he liked about her. That, and the obvious fact that, even with a black eye, she was quite attractive. That must be it—purely physical.

"I'm here alone. Isn't that enough? I can take care of myself."

"From the look of that shiner, you're not doing a very good job of it right now, are you?" He finished with his shoes and propped his elbows on widespread knees, giving her a close look.

"That's just because I got caught unawares. I won't let *that* happen again."

Darlene gave Mac a challenging look. Why was he probing her like this? Why was she resisting the truth? It was crazy, but something about this man made her want to sound better than she actually was. In truth, she'd made a mess of things.

She looked into his steady eyes. They were a clear, deep blue as opposed to her own red-rimmed, bloodshot ones. Evidently his hair was prone to curl naturally, which it began to do as it dried, softening his face with a gentle, dark frame.

Maybe Mac Jackson was a man she could trust. He had put her up for the night, and she didn't have to fight him off in the wee-morning hours. For that she was indeed grateful.

"Okay. You want to know so much, I'll tell you," she said finally. "Wiley and I were, uh, driving across the country. I liked it here and decided to stay. He didn't." There, that should hush his questions, she thought smugly.

"Is Wiley your husband?"

"No! He's my—" She halted and thought for a moment. "He's my ex."

"Ex . . . boyfriend?"

"Man. Ex-out-of-my-life man," she stated with conviction.

He nodded slowly. "So Wiley left you—"

Darlene sat up sharply. "No. I told him to leave."

He shrugged. "Okay. If you say so."

There was a moment of uneasy quiet. She wasn't telling all, and he knew it.

Darlene gestured in frustration. "I can understand how a man like you, so settled in your nice, comfortable little world, would be curious about a woman like me. A waitress. Someone who moves around. A modern-day gypsy." She folded her arms, pressing the T-shirt tightly against her firm breasts.

Mac stared at her, almost spellbound. She was right. He was fascinated by her. And right now, even with her tough, I-can-handle-anything facade, she looked about as sexy as any woman he'd ever seen. "Look, you don't have to tell me anything, Darlene. Forget it. Keep your secrets."

"No. You want to know so badly, I'll tell you the truth," she responded with a touch of anger. "I want to clear the air. I'm here in Gatlinburg, godforsaken Tennessee, because Wiley and I were finished. We argued all the time, and I couldn't see going on to New Jersey with him. After four years, nothing was going right between us. When that happens, I guess it's time to split."

"I guess," Mac said softly, leaning back in the chair. A multitude of feelings tumbled inside him. In a way, he regretted pushing Darlene to this point. He had cajoled her into admitting something very painful.

Darlene stood and began pacing and talking without the encouragement of any further questions. She related how she had traveled with Wiley, how they had taken jobs wherever they could find them, how that had been okay and fun when they were younger. Lately, though, it had been harder to keep on the move. She had been dissatisfied. Wiley had been frustrated. He had started to take it out on her in various ways.

Mac listened, his admiration for her growing as she continued. Even though she had a shiner, he could see that Darlene was no victim. She wouldn't let herself be categorized as such. And she refused to place blame. She accepted full responsibility for her predicaments—with both Wiley and Stubbs.

Mac consoled himself with the belief that she was better off without Wiley, better off here alone. But, in this town, whom did she have for support? Her family was in Arkansas, if there really was a family. A person like Darlene, who traveled around so much, probably had developed few friends. She was probably a loner.

She finished her story and sat down again. Mac's inner voice said that she only had him. A virtual stranger. He leaned forward, bracing his elbows on his knees and clasping his hands between them. "Darlene, I..."

He was overwhelmed with the urge to touch her, to take her hands and apologize for the nasty ways the world had treated her and for his own intrusion into her privacy. He wanted to reassure her that everything would be all right, that he would help. It was a crazy urge for someone like him, who never interfered with anything or anyone anymore. "I'm sorry..."

"About what?"

"Everything," he muttered inanely.

But she rejected his sympathy. "Don't be. I made the choices."

"I shouldn't have pressed you about your private life."

Darlene shrugged. "It's okay. I feel better now that I got it out in the open. And you know all about me—well, not *all,* but more than you ever bargained for." She grew serious again. "I want you to know that I wasn't drinking last night, Mac. I never drink on the job, and I don't get drunk, ever. I've seen too much of that." She was thinking more of her father than her customers.

"I know you weren't, Darlene," he said gently. "But that doesn't matter. What's important is where to go from here."

"Why, to your neighbor's for chicken dinner." Darlene stood and propped her hands on her hips. "Unless you think I'm too much for them."

"Almost." He got up and smiled. "But I think they'll like you. Ready to go, cousin? I'm starved."

She nodded and smiled. "I'm starved, too...cousin."

"COUSINS, HUH?" Ida examined Darlene closely after they'd been introduced. "Don't have much family resemblance."

"That's because we're second cousins," Mac explained.

"Maybe even third," Darlene added quickly. "Your great-uncle was my mother's second cousin by marriage, wasn't he, Mac?"

He gave her a dismayed glance, then shrugged. What else could he do?

"Then that makes you kissin' cousins, right?" a young voice piped up.

Darlene stared down at a thin, blond girl who appeared to be about eight. "No. Not that kind," she said firmly.

Disappointment showed clearly in the child's face.

Gray-haired Ida tucked her arm around the girl. "This is my granddaughter, Emma. And back in the hall is her brother, Byron."

"Hi." Darlene smiled warmly at the two kids. Brown-haired Byron appeared to be a few years older than Emma.

"Have you heard about the bear?" Emma asked excitedly.

"Bear?" Darlene's eyes widened.

"Not now, Emma," a masculine voice cajoled. "We don't want to scare the little lady off before she's even had dinner."

Darlene felt her hand being immersed in warmth as she looked up into the ruddy face of another mountain man. "You must be Boyd," she murmured. Boyd was a big man with a tinge of gray in his hair and a thick mustache. His gaze took in all of her, including the bulky, masculine clothes she wore.

"Right you are," he said affably. "And we're glad to have you here."

Darlene was urged to sit down next to Ida at the dining table.

Emma sat on her other side. "Why are you wearing Mac's clothes?" she asked boldly.

"Why, I, uh . . ." Darlene faltered, trying to think of a decent reason. Instinctively she looked at Mac.

"She fell in the creek," he answered readily. "And her other clothes are, uh, inappropriate."

"In-a-rope?" Emma repeated with a giggle. "Does that mean they're tied up somewhere?"

"Sort of," Mac replied with a laugh and a teasing tweak on Emma's cheek. "Darlene needs to get some jeans and shirts, which are more appropriate for the mountains."

The girl fixed a curious gaze on Darlene's face. "Have you been in a fight?"

Darlene touched the bruise on her face. "I did it when I fell."

"That's enough questions for one day, Emma," Boyd interjected with a scolding expression to the child. "Go help your grandmother bring in the food."

"Tell her about the bear, Daddy," Emma coaxed as she skipped away.

"It's true," Boyd admitted. "Seems several of the neighbors have spotted a black bear digging into garbage cans the last few days. Have you seen him, Mac?"

Mac shook his head.

"Does this happen often?" Darlene's dark eyes grew round.

"Well, this *is* Bear Creek," Mac explained. "At one time, it was the natural habitat for the bear—partly because of the water and abundant fish, partly because of the salt in the soil, which attracts them, too. Then, as the place became more populated, the bears left or were driven out. When a male bear reaches two years of age, he's thrown out of his mother's den. Occasionally one comes around civilization, where finding food is easier."

In spite of the unsettling news about the bear, Darlene found herself enjoying this family. She felt strangely accepted by them. Strangely, because Darlene had never felt completely accepted by any family, especially her own. Growing up had been a struggle for her. She had watched her ma and pa fuss and argue so often that it seemed natural for her to have the same kind of relationship with her older brother. Then, it had been the same with Wiley.

She'd missed family experiences like this, and as she grew older, Darlene missed her son, Ken. Quiet, shy Byron was a strong reminder of the son she'd left in Arkansas. And bold, daring Emma reminded her in some ways of her younger self. She also had an older brother and had grown up challenging his every demand. It was the only way she could remain true to herself. Otherwise, she'd have become his puppet. And Darlene could never be anybody's puppet.

Ida's time-worn face was sweet and loving, and Darlene recalled Mac's comment about how such a fine woman could have such a lousy son. Obviously she was keeping house and taking care of Boyd's children. But where was his wife—the mother of his children? No one mentioned her, and Darlene grew curious about her.

After they'd eaten more than six people should, the kids ran outside to play. The men lingered over coffee, and Darlene ached for a cigarette. To keep herself busy as well as to show her appreciation for the meal, she rose to help Ida with the dishes. When she returned to the dining room to place the "good dishes" in the china cabinet, she overheard the men's conversation.

"And if I take this job in town, I won't have time to manage the cabins," Boyd was saying. "I need someone reliable right away and wondered if you'd be interested, Mac."

"Me?"

"It's really a part-time position. Doesn't require much time. And you only have your fishing tours. I figured you could do both."

"Well, Boyd," Mac began slowly, "I'd do it, but I'm booked solid with tours every weekend. Plus, I just agreed to do the accounts for two new businesses in town."

"I understand, Mac. Maybe you know someone I could trust to manage the cabins. I could even offer that little cabin for living quarters as incentive."

Mac scratched his head. "I'll keep it in mind, Boyd."

"I could do it." Darlene surprised herself as well as the men by speaking up so abruptly. They turned to stare at her. "I'd like to do it," she said simply.

"I'm not so sure it's a job for a little lady like yourself," Boyd argued.

"That's ridiculous," Darlene scoffed. "I could handle it. I need a place to stay, anyway." She glanced at Mac. "A girl can't live with her cousin forever."

"Well, now, this is a switch," Boyd drawled. "I thought you were just here for a visit with your *cousin*."

"I'd like to stay awhile. And work," she explained.

Boyd gave Mac a little grin. "I was thinking of getting someone who could do a few repairs around the place. A man. You know?"

"What kind of repairs?" she challenged.

"Oh, painting, and fixing up after destructive renters. Sometimes we have an occasional stopped-up toilet."

"That's minor stuff," she pointed out. "I could do it."

Boyd raised one eyebrow. "Have you ever managed rentals?"

"No. But how difficult can it be?"

Obviously offended by her declarations, Boyd looked questioningly at Mac. "What do you think, Mac? Can your *little cousin* handle it?"

"Well, I, uh . . ."

Darlene was steamed, but before she or Mac had a chance to respond to Boyd, Ida entered from the kitchen. "I think she can do it, Boyd. Let her prove it."

He glanced at his mother and after a moment's hesitation, gave in to her urging. "All right. Since you're Mac's cousin, I'll give you a chance to prove it, Darlene. How soon can you start?"

"How soon can I move in?"

"Right away."

"Okay." She looked at Mac. "Let's go get my clothes." Darlene smiled to herself as she climbed into the Jeep. She had herself a new job and even a cabin to stay in. Not bad, considering the mess she'd been in only an hour ago.

MAC DROVE HER TO TOWN in stony silence. He glanced at Darlene who sat next to him, clutching the plastic bag containing her skimpy costume. What the hell was wrong with him, anyway? What difference did it make to him what she did? Or where?

That was the biggest problem. The woman did certain uncomfortable things to him, sent his blood racing and made his pulse pound. He'd been hoping to get rid of her today. But instead, she'd be living across the creek from him. That, he knew already, was too close.

A part of him wanted her out of his sight, out of his mind. Another part of him wanted to discard the impossible barriers he'd imposed on himself and haul her against him and kiss her until she stopped fighting him and the world around her.

He glanced at her again. She caught his gaze this time and smiled. Sexily tousled hair, fawnlike brown eyes, one bruised cheek on absolutely porcelain skin, a wide, very kissable mouth—she was irresistible! *Cousin, indeed!*

3

MAC PULLED HIS JEEP to a stop at the rear entrance of The Blue Boar.

Darlene gazed at the stairway with unexpected nervousness as ugly memories of the last time she'd been here resurfaced. Gathering her strength, she took a deep breath and let it out. "Okay..."

Mac sensed her hesitation. "Want me to go with you?" he offered.

"Heavens, no!" She gave him a look of disdain. "Why would I want that?"

"Look, Darlene, it's perfectly understandable for you to be a little afraid of—"

"Afraid? Me? Ha!" Her bravado sounded forced. "That's ridiculous. *I'm* not afraid of anything, especially this crummy place and its jerk of an owner."

"I'll bet," Mac agreed, sardonically pressing his lips together. "Excuse my poor choice of words." So this was the way she played the game of life, huh? Stubborn and defiant. It was almost amusing, this slip of a woman with a big bruise on her face claiming not to be afraid of anything.

"I'm independent, self-reliant and—"

"Damn stubborn," he finished. "Hey, old Stubbs is unpredictable, and he *did* rough you up a bit."

"It won't happen again. I guarantee," she replied. "Anyway, the bar should be empty this time of day, except for the couple who clean it."

"Okay. You seem to have it all figured out."

"I'll be right back," she said cheerfully and grabbed the door handle.

"Do you want me to try to find some boxes while you're gone?"

"Boxes? For what?"

"Aren't we going to move your belongings after you get your purse?"

She paused and smiled up at Mac. He obviously didn't understand her situation at all. Her shaggy hair fell gently across one shoulder as she inclined her head. "I travel light, Mac. No boxes needed."

He shrugged and let one large, tanned hand drop onto the top curve of the steering wheel. "Then I'll wait for you here."

"I'll be quick." Darlene dashed up the stairs clutching the hated costume, which she'd stuffed into a plastic bag.

Mac watched her with a wry smile. What a spitfire! She looked like Charlie Chaplin, dressed in his sloppy clothes. Her enthusiasm for the job Boyd had offered her and the new opportunity it represented was obvious. He hoped it would be everything she expected. But frankly, Mac couldn't see that working at Bear Creek Cabins was any big deal.

To Darlene, though, the "big deal" was an interesting job coupled with a place to live that was *not* connected to a bar or restaurant. Plus she'd gotten this job without any influence from Wiley. For the first time in four years she was totally liberated from his dominance, and that was a great feeling.

She pulled open the door and entered the back of the bar, expecting it to be empty. Instead, Stubbs sat at the old wooden desk, which was loaded with everything from boxes of cocktail napkins to bottles of cleaning liquid. The acrid smell of disinfectant filled the air.

He stopped punching an adding machine that was squeezed into a narrow space on the desk in front of him and gave her a slow, approving grin. "Well, hi there, sugar. I figured you wouldn't stay away for long."

Darlene took a moment to summon her nerve. She would not be intimidated or defeated by this domineering, abrasive man. "I only came back to get my purse. In case you hadn't guessed by now, I quit."

"Aw, now, don't jump the gun. Too bad you left in such a hurry last night. What happened to your pretty li'l face? Got a boo-boo?"

She gritted her teeth. "You know exactly what happened, Stubbs."

"Fell down those stairs, huh? You should be more careful, sugar."

"I'm through here, Stubbs. You can't push me around like that and get away with it. I quit." Darlene spotted her scuffed, fake-leather purse sitting amid the mess on Stubbs's desk. It was within his reach, obviously placed there after being rescued from the floor where she'd dropped it last night. She wondered if he'd gone through it and if her few dollars were still there.

"You quit?" Stubbs said mockingly. "But why, sugar? You had a good thing goin' here."

"You're wrong. I had a lousy thing going here. No wonder you can't keep waitresses, if you treat them all like you treated me."

"Just what do you think you're goin' to do in this one-horse town if you quit working here?"

"I'll find something without you." She certainly wasn't about to reveal her new job plans or where she'd be living. She didn't want Stubbs to know any more about her than he already did.

"It'll be hard to find a job. There isn't much here for someone like you." He smiled caustically. "Someone with no skills except being a waitress."

"Don't you worry about me, Stubbs. I can take care of myself." Darlene stepped closer to the desk and tossed the plastic bag onto the open ledger and adding machine on which Stubbs was working. "Here's your crummy costume."

He looked down at the bag and made no move. His stillness lulled her into thinking she could easily grab her purse—which she tried to do. But Stubbs moved quickly and clamped his hand over her wrist. "You looked so cute in this little number, sugar. I'd like to see you in it again."

"Well, you won't. Ever! Not on me or anyone. Thanks to you, it's torn." She tried to pull away, but he held her firmly. "Turn me loose!"

"Where're you goin' so fast? Stay awhile, Dar-leen."

"Let me go!"

"C'mon, honey, we can pick up where we left off last night. Again, there's no one here to bother us. The Hockleys finished cleaning early today." His eyes narrowed and he stood so he could keep his grip on Darlene as she struggled to free herself.

"Let me go or I'll—" Desperately she snatched a handle from his desk and came up with a squeegee for cleaning windows and mirrors.

"You'll what?" he asked with a laugh. "Clean my windows? Or scream! I told you, there's no one within shoutin' distance."

"Oh, yes, there is!" Mac's voice boomed from the doorway. "Do as the lady says, Stubbs. Let her go."

Startled, Stubbs loosened his tight hold. "Hey, Mac!" He chuckled self-consciously. "What are you doing here?"

Darlene jerked free. She grabbed her purse and backed out of Stubbs's reach. Then she faced Mac and snapped, "Yeah, what are you doing here?"

"Making sure he leaves you alone."

"I can do that, thank you very much."

"Sure. Like you did last night?" Mac motioned to her. "Over here."

Sullenly, Darlene moved closer to him. After all, Mac did represent safety.

Mac pointed a finger at Stubbs. "If you try to follow her or bother her in any way, I'll personally hog-tie you and haul you down to the sheriff's office to file a complaint."

"What could he do?" Stubbs folded his huge arms across his rounded belly. "It's my word against this . . . this stranger's. Nobody in town knows her, including you, Mac. Who's gonna believe her? Anyway, I didn't do anything."

"Are you saying I'm a liar?" Darlene screeched as her anger surged to an instant boil. "Why, you—" She started for him, squeegee high in the air, but Mac grabbed her arm and firmly held her.

"Hold it, Darlene," he commanded in a low voice. "Don't push your luck." Then to Stubbs, he said, "Legally, the intent for harm was there. And I'm sure we could find others who would be willing to back Darlene's story as witnesses, or with complaints of their own against you, Stubbs."

"Hogwash! Idle threats!"

"Could you stand an investigation of your business practices, Stubbs?"

"I'll bet all kinds of trouble would pop up," Darlene claimed.

Mac pushed the door open and motioned for Darlene to precede him down the stairs. "I suggest you keep your nose clean, Stubbs, and leave Darlene alone. If you know what's good for you, that is."

She tossed the squeegee behind her and dashed down the stairs. Mac backed out and slammed the door shut, then followed Darlene.

When they were both safely in the Jeep, Mac sighed heavily. Darlene glared at him. "I was surprised to see you in there."

"About as surprised as Stubbs," he agreed with a little chuckle.

"You really like shoving your weight around, don't you?"

Mac eyed her for a moment. "When it's necessary." She wasn't one bit grateful for his interference.

"Did you think that was necessary?"

"Damn right, or I wouldn't have bothered." Angrily he jerked the gearshift and started the motor with a roar. "After what happened last night, I thought you'd need a hand. When I saw Stubbs's truck in the alley, I knew he was in the bar. And I figured you didn't particularly want to meet up with him again. Somehow I thought you'd be glad to see me. Guess I figured wrong." A muscle in his jaw flexed as he steered the Jeep down the narrow alley. "What's with you, anyway?"

"I'm sure I could've handled it, that's all," Darlene insisted as they drove to her apartment a few blocks away. "I'd like to claw his eyes out!"

"I'll remember that next time."

"There won't be a next time," she retorted confidently.

"Not for me, anyway." Mac halted the Jeep at the curb with an angry jolt.

"I'll be right back." Darlene grabbed her purse and headed for the run-down building where she'd stayed for two nights. Now the idea of spending one more night here was totally repulsive.

Stubbs had made a few phone calls and gotten her the place as if he were doing her a favor. Even though she hated it, she'd had no choice but to accept at the time. But now she had somewhere else to go. She began to stuff clothes into the old duffel bag. It wouldn't take long to gather her things; there wasn't much.

Mac leaned back in the seat and sighed heavily. What the heck was wrong with him? Was he mad because she didn't want his help? That made no sense. Why didn't he just save them both this trouble and butt out?

For some reason he couldn't quite understand, Mac decided to follow her into the apartment building. Something about her drew him. Perhaps she roused some stupid protective feelings that he managed to keep hidden most of the time. Maybe it was her rebellious attitude that attracted him. Or was it the fact that she was a challenge? By the time he reached her, Darlene was smoking a cigarette with one hand and cramming clothes into an aged duffel bag with the other.

"I... uh, I forgot to thank you," she said hesitantly. "I don't know what got into me back there. I do appreciate what you did, Mac. It's just that I've never had anybody fight my battles for me, and I didn't know how to act. Guess that's another one I owe you."

"You don't owe me anything, Darlene." Mac felt uncomfortable with her humble attitude. He wasn't sure he even liked this meeker version of her.

She paused and smiled at him. "Oh? Are you like Batman, going around doing good for no reason?"

He folded his arms and leaned against the door frame, watching her juggle clothes and the cigarette. Even with a contrite expression, she could still zing him. "I still feel a little responsible for you. God knows why. I guess it's because I just happened to be there."

She propped one fist on her hip. "Yeah, and I just happened to get lucky for once in my life." Mac Jackson was one unusual man, and meeting him was one of the few lucky breaks she'd ever had. So why did she keep fighting him?

He gestured at her cigarette. "You'd better be careful with that thing. You might burn something."

"I've been smoking long enough to know how to handle a cigarette," she replied with an arrogant flick of her wrist.

"How long is that?"

"Ten years. Since I was sixteen." She blew smoke into the air.

"Well, when you were sixteen, I doubt that you were very concerned about what cigarettes could do to your insides. But now that you're all grown up, you should know they're bad for you."

She frowned. "I can do without your lecture on the evils of smoking."

He shrugged. "I can see that it wouldn't do any good, so I won't waste my effort. Anyway, I'll bet you couldn't stop smoking at this point."

"I can do anything I want to," she bragged and stubbed the cigarette out in a small ashtray.

"Oh, really?" he challenged.

"*If* I wanted to."

"But not if you're hooked."

"Hooked?" She made a face.

"Or addicted."

"I am not addicted!" She zipped the duffel bag. "That sounds so . . . criminal."

"You *are* addicted. That's why you wanted a cigarette so badly when you couldn't get your hands on one."

"I just wanted one, that's all." She folded her arms and tapped one toe. "Look, could we just get going and leave my bad habits alone?"

"Sure." He reached for the bag. "Is this everything?"

"I told you I travel light." She sailed out of the room in front of him.

They arrived at Bear Creek just before dark. Mac walked her to the front door of the Blevinses' house. He felt an obligation to deliver her to her destination. No . . . If he admitted the truth, he just didn't want to leave her yet.

Ida greeted them with a broad, welcoming smile. "Well, that was quick. Did you get everything?"

"I didn't have much," Darlene explained. She winked at Emma, who peered curiously from beside her grandmother.

"Is that all?" the child asked shyly. "One little suitcase? I have more than that."

"Makes it easier for me to travel. Why do I need more?" Darlene responded tartly. The nerve of that kid annoyed her.

"Aren't you going to stay here very long?"

Darlene shrugged. "Depends."

"Hush your questions, child," Ida admonished. She took Darlene's arm and gently pulled her into the living room. "She hasn't even started the job yet. Give her a chance to like it. She might just decide to stay here awhile."

Mac set the duffel bag just inside the door. "Well, uh, if you don't need me anymore, I'll be going."

"This is fine, Mac. I'll show her the office cabin." Ida told him.

"Okay." He shifted from one foot to the other. "Well, see you later."

Darlene turned toward him as he stepped back out onto the porch. Mixed emotions tumbled around inside her. They were all so fresh and new and different. "Mac, thanks," she said softly, meeting his gaze with sincerity. "Thanks for everything. I owe you—"

He shook his head modestly and raised one palm. "Nope. It was nothing."

She grinned and tossed her head saucily. "Well, then, thanks for nothing."

"Anytime." He shrugged. "If you need a ride into town for anything, let me know."

"Will you come to visit me in my new place?"

"You want me to?" For a moment, he felt like a smitten schoolboy. He stuffed his hands into his pockets and looked down at her.

"Sure. We'll be neighbors, won't we?" She smiled and waved her fingers. Quietly she added, "Kissin' cousins, right?"

"Yeah." Mac's mouth went dry, and he realized there was nothing else to say. He could only think of how he wanted to kiss her. And not a peck on the cheek, either.

Abruptly he wheeled around and lowered his shaggy head as he walked rapidly toward the Jeep. For some weird reason, he hated to leave Darlene, even though he knew she was in good hands with Ida. If he had any ridiculous notions of protection, he may as well forget it. She had made it perfectly clear she didn't want anything from him—except maybe a visit.

These thoughts were absolutely crazy! He'd gotten himself into hot water more than once with his meddling, superprotective actions. Hadn't he learned his lesson?

Since coming to Gatlinburg, Mac had made new rules for his life and followed them to the T until Darlene had shown up on his doorstep. He was still vulnerable. And he wouldn't let that happen. So, he had to keep her in her place . . . at least at arm's length. Or more. He drove away without looking back.

CARRYING HER DUFFEL BAG, Darlene followed Ida down the short path to the cabin that doubled as an office. The gravel road swung around past the house, where a broken sign directed guests to stop at the first cabin to make their arrangements.

Once they were inside, Ida waved at the desk as she walked past it. "I'll explain all this tomorrow."

Darlene noticed a typewriter alongside the phone on the desk. Did knowing how to type go along with the job? "I can't type, Ida. Do I need to?"

"It would help. But if you can't, no problem. Just do what I do. The H 'n' P system works fine."

"H and P system?" Darlene looked puzzled. "What's that?"

"Hunt 'n' peck," Ida said with a chuckle. "Search and you will find!"

"That's pretty slow," Darlene remarked dubiously.

Ida opened a narrow closet filled with linens and toiletries and seized some towels, sheets, pillowcases and soap. "You can use these. They're for the guests and are always clean and ready. If they want more than the room supply, here is where you get them. We only have two guests right now. Should have more with all that's going on in town. But Boyd has let the cabins go until they're a wreck. Can't rent 'em if the toilets don't flush.

But we'll get into that later, too." She pushed the door that led into the back section of the cabin and switched on a lamp. "Such as it is, here's home."

With the word *home* flickering around in her mind, Darlene walked into one large room. A kitchen at one end and a bed at the other were separated by a small dining table. Beside the bed was a worn, stuffed chair. "Nice. . . ." she murmured.

"It's not great, but it's sufficient. There's a large porch all across the back with a pretty view of the woods," Ida explained. "And tomorrow I'll get you some pots and pans for the kitchen. Nobody's lived here for a long time. When I ran the cabins, I used that table for sewing, as well as doing the books."

"You managed the cabins?"

"Oh, yes. But it got to be too much for me to do this and take care of the kids, too. We've tried to get people to help, but it just hasn't worked out."

"I'll do a good job for you," Darlene promised. She was determined to make this work. She needed the money desperately, and from what she could see, this sure beat restaurant work.

"I know you'll do fine," Ida agreed, dropping the folded sheets on the bed. She stepped inside the small bathroom to hang the towels and emerged with a hopeful smile. "Well, what do you think? I know it needs lots of work. But can you stand it here?"

"You know something, Ida?" Darlene said softly as she walked slowly around the room. "I think it's finer than most anyplace I've ever lived."

"It couldn't be," Ida disagreed. "This is so. . .rough."

"But it is. I like it here. Kind of reminds me of back home in Arkansas." Only this cabin had no cracks between the logs and was probably lots warmer in winter than the old family house. She spied a large stone fireplace at one end near the bed and walked toward it.

"We have firewood for all the cabins," Ida told her. "We'll stack some for you, for the cool nights."

Darlene smiled and hugged her arms excitedly. She really liked this cabin a lot.

Ida adjusted the tattered curtains. "It's not very fancy, but with some fixing, it could be okay."

"It could be very nice." Darlene eagerly helped Ida make the bed. She smoothed the sheets with her hand, relishing their clean-smelling fragrance.

"I'm afraid there's no TV here. None of the cabins have TVs. We figure folks don't come up here to watch the tube. But I'm sure we can get you one."

Darlene shrugged. "I'm not used to having one. It doesn't matter."

Ida went to a large closet, pulled out a brightly colored patchwork quilt and spread it on the bed. "There are plenty of blankets in the closet in case you get cold. Don't mind my sewing mess in the bottom. I'll move it out of your way tomorrow."

Darlene peered into the closet. "Is that your sewing machine?"

"It's my old one. Boyd and the kids gave me a fancy new one last Christmas. Do you sew?"

"Sometimes." Darlene hadn't been able to sew since she'd sold her machine so Wiley could buy his saddle before their trip out west. She hadn't realized how much she'd miss it.

"Use this one, if you want," Ida offered generously. "I did lots of sewing out here before Sammi Jo—Emma and Byron's mom—left. My friend and I were going to start a business." She sighed heavily. "But things changed. Mary Beth had to go live with her daughter in Knoxville, and I got too busy to sew anything except repairing the kids' clothes and occasionally making something for Emma."

"What happened to the kids' mother?" Darlene asked, curious.

"Sammi Jo was Boyd's second wife. The first one was a disaster, too, but that's another story. You'll know soon enough, so I might as well tell you now. One day, Sammi Jo just left. We got a postcard from her a few weeks later from California. I don't know what got into that girl. She left her kids and husband high and dry."

Darlene felt a knot grip her stomach. She wanted to be shocked, but the story was too familiar. Turning her face away, she wondered if Ida could see her guilt.

"So that's when I took over full-time with the kids. Anyway," Ida continued, "you can use anything in that box. It's full of material I never got around to using. There may be enough to make curtains if you're interested. That was always my intent. Course, I never got to it."

"What's this?" Darlene pulled at something tucked behind the box that resembled a pair of feet.

"Oh, that." Ida chuckled. "It's one of my dolls that I never finished. You can work on her if you want."

Darlene looked at the dangling form. "I wouldn't know where to start."

"The hardest part of that one's been done. She's already stuffed. She needs hair. And clothes. And a face." Ida sighed. "If you're interested, I'll show you how someday."

"I've never made a doll."

"It's easy. And fun. They kind of take on a little personality. I know that sounds crazy." She rubbed her hands together. "Well, that's about it. If you need anything else, Darlene, please let me know."

Darlene held on to the doll. "This is fine. Better than fine, believe me."

"Since you don't have any kitchen utensils yet, why don't you come over in the morning for breakfast?"

"Oh, I couldn't—"

"I fix breakfast for the kids every morning. It'd be no trouble to throw another egg in the pot."

"No egg. Just, uh . . ."

"Buttermilk biscuits?"

"Well, maybe one."

"Is that all? No wonder you're so skinny," Ida commented with a serious nod at Darlene's figure. "And coffee?"

"Well, maybe just a cup."

"Okay. Come on over anytime. We get up early. After breakfast, I'll show you how I run the office. Now, if you need anything, just call."

"Ida . . . thanks for the job. And everything here."

"It isn't much, girl." Ida gave her a stern look. "But I expect honest work from Mac's cousin. And I'm sure you're someone I can trust. That's why I hired you."

"I, uh—" Darlene stammered at the mention of honesty. "Ida, I have to tell you—"

"What, honey?"

"Mac and I aren't—" She hesitated. Would this confession ruin a good thing? "We aren't related. We aren't really cousins."

Ida laughed. "I've known that all along. I can tell by the way you look at him. And by the way he looks at you!"

"Oh, no. There's nothing between us. He hardly knows me, and I—" If she revealed too much, it could jeopardize her job. "Well, I'm not interested. That's all."

"I see things, girl. I've been around a few years, y'know."

"I'll work hard for you, Ida," Darlene firmly declared.

"I believe it, honey. Have a good night, now, and we'll see you in the morning."

When she was alone, Darlene returned to the office. The typewriter here was older than the one at Mac's. But it would give her a chance to learn typing. She'd like that. Then she could type letters to Ken regularly. They could begin to communicate, as a mother and son should. She would never—*could never*—leave her child completely, the way Sammi Jo had done. How awful it must be for Emma and Byron.

Back in her large one-room "apartment," Darlene pulled out the letter she'd written to Ken earlier and placed it on the table to remind herself to get an envelope and stamp tomorrow. She sat on the edge of the bed and surveyed the plain room. As Ida had said, there certainly was potential for fixing it up. That was something she could do. Seemed as if she was always fixing up her life, so what was one room?

Today she had been given an opportunity for a new start. No more restaurants or bars. Learning to type was a new challenge. She wouldn't be satisfied with Ida's H 'n' P system. She was tired of fighting her way through life—struggling with everything. She was going to make something of herself.

Perhaps here, working for some nice folks, was a good place to begin the changes she wanted in her life. With effort, she could make this cabin into a decent home—one Ken would be proud to visit. Oh, that would be great!

Darlene tossed the doll aside and reached for a cigarette. It was the last one in the pack, and she began scrambling through her duffel bag for another pack before she even lit this one. None. She plopped down again and sighed heavily.

Suddenly Mac's words taunted her: *Bet you can't quit.* "Bet I can," she said aloud, startling herself. Damn Mac, anyway. He was one aggravating man. He reminded her of her brother, Chase—Mr. Supreme Macho Know-It-All.

"I'll show you, Mac," she challenged, fingering the cigarette. "I'll quit and show you, Mac Jackson!" She lifted the cigarette to her lips. "Tomorrow."

As she lit up, Darlene knew she had another fight on her hands.

4

DARLENE SPENT MOST of the next week learning to be manager of the six Bear Creek cabins and battling her constant urge for a cigarette. Battling it every waking moment. She even woke up one night, craving a smoke. Most of the time, though, she won. Occasionally, the habit won.

She devoted her spare time to cleaning and fixing up the cabin. As she worked, it began to feel like a place of her own. This was something she'd never had, never even had any motivation to have. She had always been stuck in some cheap, ugly apartment. But here, in this quaint and potentially lovely cabin, her nesting instincts were reawakened, and she wanted to make this *her* home.

She was just adding the finishing touches to new curtains one afternoon when Ida and Emma appeared at her door.

"This is purely a social call," Ida began primly. "No business. Nothing about the cabins or leaky faucets or toilets that don't flush. It's just a neighborly visit." Ida thrust a warm casserole dish into Darlene's hands. "Welcome to the Bear Creek community."

Darlene stood in the open doorway, stunned for a moment by the show of kindness. No one had ever welcomed her to a neighborhood. There had been no casseroles, no "I'm so glad you're here." It was always "Here it is. Rent's due on the first."

She followed her guests into the room. "Excuse my mess, but I've been sewing. I didn't expect company."

"We're not company. We're neighbors. There's a difference—you'll see," Ida advised.

"These are for you," Emma said, sticking out a fistful of wildflowers.

"Why, thank you, Emma. How lovely." Darlene took her housewarming gifts to the kitchen counter. She stuffed the flowers into a glass and added water from the faucet. "They'll brighten the room and remind me of you. Emma—all fresh and beautiful."

Emma beamed proudly. "I picked them, myself, on the way over here."

Ida approached the sewing machine on the kitchen table, which was surrounded by various bits of scattered fabric. "I see you're sewing. What are you making, Darlene?"

"I made these curtains." Darlene gestured at the windows. "Hope you don't mind that I used some of the material in that box you left in the closet."

"Of course, I don't mind," Ida assured her. "I told you to use whatever you wanted."

Ida stood in the middle of the room, hands on her plump hips, and gazed with frank approval. "Darlene, I can't believe the changes you've made in this place in the short time you've been here. Everything looks so homey and settled."

"Think so? I just cleaned it a bit," Darlene responded modestly. She was proud of the way the place was shaping up, too.

"Your curtains even match the quilt design. How clever!"

"Well, there wasn't enough of one kind of material, so I did what my grandma used to do—patched it together." *Like my life,* she thought grimly. Darlene felt as if everything she had done until now had been a hodgepodge, a patchwork of events, strewn together with no sense of purpose. "Grandma called it Jacob's Coat. It was her favorite pattern because she could use up all her scraps."

"My mother used that pattern in her quilts, too. In fact, she made the one on your bed." Ida walked over and caressed the cover with a gentle, loving touch. "As much as I love to sew, I've never made a quilt. Never had the time."

"Me, too. Please, have a seat." Darlene gestured toward the stuffed chair near the bed. "Would you like coffee? Or how about some spiced tea?"

"That sounds good. I haven't had spiced tea in ages."

"Can I have some, too?" Emma asked.

"Sure." Darlene set the kettle on the stove and reached for a couple of tea bags. "Here . . . smell. This one's orange spice. Do you like it?"

Emma sniffed, then looked up at Darlene with admiration shining in her eyes. "Yeah. Neat!"

"Can I help?" Ida offered.

"No, you just have a seat, Ida." Darlene pointed to the chair. "I'm the hostess this time, and I'll serve. You've served me plenty of times this week in your kitchen. Now it's my turn."

Darlene was surprised by how comfortable and friendly she felt toward Ida and Emma. She'd had to leave every friend she'd ever made because Wiley had been constantly on the move and she was the dutiful companion who'd followed him. She hadn't realized how much fun another female friend could be. Sipping tea and chatting and laughing with Ida like old acquaintances was her first chance in the longest time to develop a real friendship.

"I can't tell you how good it is to have you as my neighbor," Ida said. "Mary Beth and I had lots of fun together before she moved to Knoxville. Now, we're so far away from each other, we don't get to visit much at all. Only by phone."

"They talk for hours!" Emma piped in.

"No, not that long."

"You must miss her," Darlene remarked sympathetically.

"Sure do. Now, my closest neighbor is Mac. And although he's fine, he's . . . a man."

Darlene laughed, thinking of the very masculine Mac Jackson. "He's that, all right."

"Well, you know what I mean." Ida blushed. "I couldn't drop in for a cup of hot tea with him!"

"Oh, I don't know," Darlene teased. "He seems to be a nice, friendly type." *Friendly enough to let me spend the night when he hardly knew me!*

"Oh, he's a good man. Not exactly the tea-sipping type, but solid." She paused to take a drink of her tea. "Have you, uh, seen him this week?"

"No." Darlene fingered the handle of her cup and tried not to sound too disappointed. "I'm sure he's been too busy. And so have I."

"I'll bet he'd love to see you. Why don't you just walk over there? It isn't far by the back trail."

"You have to walk the rocks to cross the stream," Emma said. "Once I fell in and got soaking wet."

"I grew up beside a river. I've had my share of dunkings, too," Darlene responded with a little smile.

"Did your brother pull you out, too?"

"Well, yes. Matter of fact, he did," Darlene admitted. "More than once."

"You must understand by now that Mac is something of a loner," Ida went on, taking a sip of tea. "He's a fine man but doesn't have much to do with folks. Except us, of course. Now, in my day, if I wanted to get a young man's attention, I'd bake him a pie."

"Who said I was trying to get his attention?" Darlene stiffened. "Are you trying to play Cupid, Ida?"

"I happen to know that his favorite is cherry pie."

"I make shoe-leather crust."

"Then make him something you do well." Ida gestured at the windows. "Like new kitchen curtains. I believe there's some brown-and-white checked material in the bottom of the box that would be nice in his house. Use it."

Darlene felt nervous talking about Mac and reached into the bedside-table drawer for a cigarette. "I don't care to get his attention, Ida. And making him curtains is out of the question. I'm much too busy to bother." Before she could light the cigarette, she remembered her attempt to quit smoking and, with a shake of her head, tossed the cigarette onto the little table. "I'm trying to quit," she explained. "It's hard."

Ida patted her hand. "Quitting smoking is the best thing you could do for yourself, honey."

"It may be the hardest, too," Darlene observed with a little chuckle. "But it's one battle I'm determined to win."

"Good girl! Stick to your guns."

"That's one reason I've been able to do so much this week. I've tried to keep myself busy every minute." She glanced at the kitchen table where Emma was picking through the scraps Darlene had left from her sewing.

"Can I have some of these, Darlene?" Emma asked, waving a few choice pieces of material.

"Sure. Take anything you want."

Emma looked at her grandmother. "We can use them for Sammi, can't we, Gran?"

Ida nodded. "We'll make her some curtains like Darlene's."

"Sammi?" Darlene asked softly, glancing at Ida. "Her mother?"

"Her doll," Ida told her in a whisper.

Glad to have the conversation diverted from Mac, Darlene went over to the table and began helping Emma find the largest pieces of material. "Sammi's your doll's name?"

"Gran made her for me," Emma answered solemnly. "She's beautiful. Plus, she's my best friend."

"I had a doll like that once. A best friend." *My only one,* Darlene thought ruefully. She handed Emma a brightly colored piece of Paisley. "Remember I have an older brother, just like you do."

Emma cocked her head. "Did you fight with him, too?"

"Oh, we did our share, I guess," Darlene replied. "He always tried to boss me. And I never liked that."

"Me, too!" Emma propped her small fists on her hips. "Byron thinks he's Mr. Know-It-All. And he's not."

Darlene laughed. "That's exactly what I called my brother, Chase. But, you know something neat?" She sat down and gazed at Emma on eye level. "When we grew up, he became a pretty good guy. And we're friends now."

Emma stuck out her lip. "Byron will never be my friend. Sammi is my only friend. And Gran."

"Well, I'd like to be your friend," Darlene offered, handing Emma a strip of lovely lace. "You can come to visit me anytime you want. And bring Sammi along. I'd like to meet her."

"Okay," Emma agreed. "Her full name's Sammi Jo." She ran to Ida to show her the material she'd gathered. "Pretty, huh, Gran?"

"Very nice, honey." Ida wrapped an arm affectionately around her granddaughter and looked up at their hostess. "This has been a pleasant little visit, Darlene. The tea was great, and now we'd better be going. We hope you'll want to stay with us for a long, long time."

"We'll see." Then, with a grin, Darlene added, "So far, I like it here—especially the neighbors." She had never stayed long in one place, so the concept was somewhat alien to her. It was something others did, but not her. And no one, until now, had cared.

Ida walked toward the door, chatting amiably. "I'm glad to see that you like to sew. Every cabin needs repairs of some kind."

"I'd love to fix them up."

"Maybe next week we can go into town and get some material for a new project for cabin three. It's a shambles since those college kids rented it for a week."

"Fine. Anytime."

Ida watched Emma skip onto the porch out of earshot and shook her head sadly. "I hope she doesn't pester you too much. She's a very lonely child since her mama left."

"She's no problem." Darlene had felt a powerful empathy for Emma. "How long's her mama been gone?"

"Two years. One day she just disappeared. Some say she ran off with a man. All I know is that she left two kids who needed someone to care for them. That's when I came to live with them. Boyd couldn't do it by himself. Anyway, he was devastated for a while. I didn't want them to lose their mother and their home at the same time, so I've been doing my best to keep it all together."

Darlene's stomach knotted—the story hit too close to home. Ida, much like her own dear mother, had picked up the pieces of their shattered lives. "You're a remarkable woman, Ida. And a very good grandmother. The kids are lucky to have you. So am I. Thanks for the welcoming party. And the casserole. Thank you, Emma, for the beautiful flowers!" she called and waved to the child, who was hopping down the steps, clutching her scraps as if they were precious. "Come back and visit anytime."

Ida turned to go, then stopped and whispered, "I'm sure he could use some new curtains. Take a look at those brown checks. Very masculine." With a girlish giggle, she was gone.

Darlene shook her head and laughed off Ida's suggestion.

When she was alone again, she thought of her own eleven-year-old son, Ken, and wondered if he had fantasies of her the way Emma did of her absent mother—always wondering where she was and if she loved him. There was a big difference, she consoled herself, between her situation and Emma's mother's. She hadn't disappeared entirely from Ken's life. She was staying in touch and reminding him that she loved him. Why, just this week, she'd received an answer to her typed letter to him. She intended to get her life in order and to make him proud of her in some way. She *would!*

In the meantime, he had a very good home with her brother, Chase, and his new wife, Suzanna. They loved him, she was sure of it. And he was happy with them. He had told her so, himself.

Darlene watched her guests—no, they were her neighbors; there was a difference. She watched her neighbors retreat down the path to the big house. She'd never been so welcomed anywhere she'd lived. Most folks were glad to see her and Wiley go, and did nothing nice to encourage them to stay another day—including her own brother!

She ambled over to the table and began gathering up the remaining scraps of fabric. She glanced into the box, which was lying open. There was the brown-and-white-checkered material Ida had mentioned. Darlene inspected it closely. Good quality. The top rows could be smocked for an unusual effect instead of gathering. . . .

* * *

"HAVE YOU SEEN THE BEAR?" Danny opened the storage room on Mac's back porch and dipped a bucket into a bin of grain.

Mac shook his head and continued pouring lead into molds for his fly-fishing lures. "Nope. But Boyd Blevins has. So be sure not to leave any scraps of food lying around when you feed your critters. We don't want to attract him."

"Right. I'm trying a different grain with the deer since he doesn't seem to like anything I bring. That broken leg will never heal if he doesn't eat. Think he'll like this sorghum grain?"

Mac shrugged. "How should I know what deer like? Whatever you do sounds good to me."

Danny took the bucket of grain to the far corner of Mac's property where it jutted against the national forest. There they'd built a pen for the larger animals Danny found, like this young deer. Next he fed the raccoon, which was caged in back of the garage. He returned to sit on the end of the porch and watch Mac pour lead into the molds. "Guess what, Mac? I think I can release the coon in a few days."

"I agree. It's time for him to go before he thinks he's tame," Mac advised. "The way he looks now, you'd never guess he got caught in a trap. Why, when you brought him in with that mangled paw, I thought surely he'd die from shock, or at the very least be severely crippled. But you fixed him up almost as good as new."

Danny beamed with pride. "I couldn't do anything if you didn't let me keep them here, Mac. My pa thinks it's dumb to spend so much time on animals."

"Well, he's a businessman, and from that standpoint he's probably right." Mac proceeded to line up his newly made lures on the worktable. "But some folks think there's more to life than strictly business."

"I sure do. I'd die if I thought I had to work like he does for the rest of my life," Danny said passionately.

"Now, Danny, don't be too hard on your dad. He has a good business. Anyway, it takes all kinds to make the world."

"Running a motel isn't *my* world," Danny grumbled.

"I understand." Mac began to clean up his paraphernalia. "Why don't you release your coon down by the creek tomorrow?"

"Okay. I've got to come back daily so I can keep a close eye on the deer until he's eating better."

"You'll figure out something for him, Danny. You always do." Mac wiped his hands on his jeans, then propped them on his hips. "Give him time. He'll come around. Your strays always do."

"What about the one I found in the alley last week? *Your* stray, Mac." Danny gave Mac a devilish grin. "Has *she* come around?"

Mac shrugged nonchalantly. "If you're talking about Darlene, I haven't seen her since she started working at Blevins's cabins last week." He had tried to force her completely out of his thoughts, but those defiant brown eyes of hers had returned to haunt him at odd times. Like now.

"Well, Mac, *I* always check on my critters."

"Darlene's not my critter," Mac corrected. "She's very much her own person. Why don't you mind your own business, kid?" He gathered a box of equipment and headed for the back door. "You know, Danny, I'd love for you to stay and talk, but I'm real busy today. Just don't have time for chitchat."

"Sensitive subject, Mac?"

"No. Just busy."

"Sure, Mac." Danny chuckled and waved as he started across the yard. "See ya tomorrow."

"Yeah, Danny." Mac hurried inside and slammed the door. He paced the floor a few times before stopping in the middle of the living room. He ran his hand around the back of his head, wondering what in the world had gotten into him. Why was he so angry? He couldn't stand to think about Darlene, didn't want to talk about her, had made no effort to see her and didn't plan to, yet couldn't get her out of his mind. That casual blond hair and those unusually dark eyes would not leave his mind.

Darlene Clements was definitely a woman to remember. *But,* Darlene was as lost as he was, perhaps more so. She was alone in a strange land—all the more reason for him to just check in on her and see how she was doing. Maybe in a few days.

THE NEXT DAY, Darlene folded up her gift, stuffed it into a plastic bag along with Mac's jeans and T-shirt, and made her way down the back path to the stream. There was a jittery feeling in the pit of her stomach at the thought of seeing Mac again. She pictured his wonderful, clear-sky-colored eyes crinkling into a smile when he saw what she'd made for him.

She recalled his whisker-shadowed chin and the way his white teeth contrasted with the brown beard. Her memory of those strong, broad shoulders made her quicken her step. She longed to see him again; to hear his voice and his husky laughter.

She heard the hissing rush of the water before she reached Bear Creek. Standing at the edge, Darlene paused and took a deep breath. Large stones, spaced just right for stepping, crudely bridged the creek.

Mustering all her courage, she stepped on the first rock. White ruffles of water circled each stepping stone. She tried not to notice. She felt slightly dizzy watching the swirling water. One step at a time, she told herself sternly.

She took a deep breath and, clutching her package to her breast, placed one foot on the next stone. She wobbled, then regained her balance and stood very still, one foot on one rock, the other foot on the next one. She hesitated. A mistake! She had to keep going. It was the only way. For a moment, she wondered if she would be stuck here forever, not able to move.

No, she had to do this. If Emma could walk these rocks, *she* could. But Emma had fallen in....

Another step. Another stone. Another— She faltered, then found her footing. Darlene's heart was racing. What if she fell into this swirling pool? Who would pull her out? She halted again, feet spread apart, trying to keep her precarious balance, trying not to watch the water, trying not to fall into the swirling dark depths of— "Hey!" she said aloud, encouraging herself. "You're all right. Keep going. Don't stop." Darlene took another unsteady step.

There were only three more rocks to go before she would be on solid ground. Why had she ever let Ida persuade her to come this way? She wouldn't return here for a million bucks. She'd walk back by the road even if it was a ten-mile hike! She didn't care. Right now, she just wanted to be on safe, solid, terra firma.

She was almost there. Then, out of nowhere, a raccoon appeared on the next stepping-stone. She waved one arm at the creature. "Get out of here!"

Amazingly bold, the mask-faced animal started toward her. Darlene yelped and tried to get out of its way. But, of course, there was nowhere to go except—into the water. She screamed. On her way down into the black, swirling depths, she thought she saw a glimpse of Mac's bearded face. *Her fantasy. . . Mac was always there to rescue her.* But it all happened so fast, she couldn't tell fantasy from reality.

Ice-cold water engulfed her, and Darlene thrashed her arms and legs, kicking and screaming with all her might. She took in a mouthful of water, gulped it down. Coughing and spluttering, she tried to scream again. Suddenly, strong steel bands wrapped around her arms, binding her, holding her, lifting her. She struggled to get free, to keep from being sucked under that black water.

"Be still!" she heard someone bellow. "I've got you!"

"Help!" she sputtered. "I'm drowning!"

"No, you're not!"

"I—can't—swim!" she gasped, feeling panicky. But somewhere her brain registered that while her feet were still in the water, her head was out of it. She could breathe.

"I figured as much," he said gruffly. "All you have to do here is stand up. You won't drown here."

Something compelled her to obey him. She stopped struggling. Water swirled around her knees. Shaken to the core, Darlene looked up into the strong face of Mac Jackson.

"You okay now?" His arms encircled her. They were the bands she'd felt. Strong. Secure. There for her.

Darlene blinked and realized that she'd fallen into a knee-deep pool. She felt like the biggest fool in the world. "When my head went under, I thought I was a goner," she murmured. Her hair dripped around her face and shoulders. She was completely soaked. A shiver ran through her. The mountain stream was icy cold.

"All you had to do was stand up." He glared at her in exasperation. "Instead, you floundered around like a beached whale. A wild one, at that. I thought you were going to drown both of us for a minute."

"Sorry. I thought so, too." She tugged at one wet sleeve of her T-shirt. "Thanks for saving me, Mac. Seems you're always bailing me out of something."

"I just happened to be here," he explained gruffly, taking her hand. Together they began sloshing toward the shore.

"Oh, no!" She halted and began looking around in the water. "Where's the package! I'll bet it's soaked! Or lost!"

"What?"

"I was carrying a package and it fell in the water, too. Please help me find it, Mac."

They searched until he found it. "Here." Mac lifted a soggy mess that had been caught between two rocks. "Is this what you're looking for?"

"Thank goodness it stayed together." She smiled at him. "It's for you."

He looked at her curiously as he pulled her out of the stream. "For me? What is it?"

"Remember the clothes you let me wear last week? And...a gift." She turned away, suddenly embarrassed by the whole situation. "If it hadn't been for that crazy raccoon trying to get me, I'd have made it across those darned rocks. I was almost there."

"Raccoon?" Mac started laughing. "So that's where he went!"

"Where *who* went? He was after me!"

"He was looking for food. He's been caged for weeks and is accustomed to someone bringing goodies. He probably thought you had something for him."

"Yeah, *me!*" she exclaimed.

"Naw. He wouldn't hurt you." Mac tucked a huge arm around her and led her down the path. "You see, Danny has been taking care of a wounded raccoon at my place and now that he's all healed, we let him go a few hours ago. The raccoon disappeared, and Danny left. It's a good thing I was trying out my new lures and heard you. Hold it a minute. This is where I left my fishing gear." He veered off the path and returned with his fishing rod, which he'd apparently dropped when he heard her.

"I was so scared, I could have drowned in that three-foot-deep pool," Darlene continued, then walked along quietly for a few minutes before admitting, "I'm deathly afraid of water."

"So I gathered." He tucked his arm around her again. Their wet clothes were cold by now, and the casual touching seemed to bring them a little warmth.

She felt better. "I realize that I panicked. But I couldn't help it. I never learned to swim, even though I grew up beside a river in Arkansas."

"You must have had some trauma to give you that kind of fear. What happened?"

"One time I was wading in a murky area of the lake where the bottom was unstable. I stepped into an underwater hole and went in over my head. That experience scared the bejesus out of me. I guess the fear has never left me."

"It's a shame you never learned to swim. It isn't too late, you know."

"You think you could teach me to swim?"

"I could."

"No, thanks. I have no desire to learn. My solution is to simply stay away from water."

"Then you're doomed to repeat this."

"No, I won't. Because I won't go near those rocks again."

"Suit yourself. But it means something has conquered you that you have the power to conquer yourself."

They walked on in silence with Darlene stewing over what Mac had said. She didn't like to be bested by anything and he knew it. Still, she had too many other hurdles without worrying about swimming, too.

They reached the porch and, at Darlene's urging, Mac unwrapped the soggy package right there. He lifted the brown-and-white check material. "What is it?"

She tingled with anticipation. "Spread it out. You'll see."

He stretched the fabric to arm's length. "Curtains?"

"You got it," Darlene replied. "Ida said you could use some kitchen curtains. You've been so nice to me, I didn't know how to repay you."

"You didn't have to repay me." His voice was low and a little gruff.

"And now I owe you another one for saving my life." She sighed and hugged her arms. "Ida suggested cherry pie, but I figured you'd like my curtains much better than my pie."

"You *made* these?"

"Of course. If you'd ever come to visit me, you'd see that I made some for my cabin, too."

"Well, thanks, Darlene. No one's ever made me curtains before. These will look great in my house." He tried not to pay attention to the way her wet T-shirt clung to her slender frame and full, well-formed breasts. He tried to ignore the dark nipples pouting acutely against the thin material. But he wasn't entirely successful.

"I hope they fit."

"What?" He could only think of the way those breasts would *feel,* warm and pliant against him.

"The curtains. I hope they fit your windows. I had no way of measuring. But I think I made a fairly good estimate."

"I'm sure they'll fit," he muttered. "We'd better get you dry. Wait here. I'll be right back." He returned in a minute with a large towel. "Peel off your clothes. Wrap yourself in that. And I'll stick your clothes in the dryer."

She unsnapped her jeans and slid the zipper down. "You planning to help me?"

He blinked and realized he'd been standing there, watching her . . . anticipating the gorgeous inevitable. "Huh? No, er, sorry. I'll change, too." He started to go, then paused. "You want to wear some of my clothes?"

She grinned. "The last time I tried them on, they didn't fit worth beans. I'll just wear this towel until mine dry, thanks."

In a few minutes, Darlene was huddled on Mac's sofa, wrapped in the large towel he'd provided. He returned wearing bleached jeans and a well-worn shirt and handed her a cup of hot chocolate.

She took the cup eagerly. "This is great." He raised the beer in his hand.

"Would you rather have a beer?"

"No, thanks. This is fine."

Mac took a seat opposite her, and they sat quietly sipping for a few minutes. "You know something?" he said finally. "You're amazing. I've never known anyone like you, Darlene. Everything you do is . . . lively."

"Or big trouble," she reminded.

"I must admit, you seem to attract it like a magnet," he agreed with a laugh and took another swig of beer. "Tell me, how's the job? Do you like managing the cabins?"

"I love it!" Darlene beamed. Her eyes brightened as she began to talk about her new job, which had also become her new life-style. "This is the best job I've ever had. It isn't really hard, just demanding. You have to be there when the guests need or want you. In that way, it's sort of like yours, Mac."

"You don't mind the work?" His gaze wandered to her bare thigh when she shifted positions.

"You mean cleaning the cabins?" She shook her head and the towel slipped to reveal one smooth shoulder. "This isn't nearly as bad as cleaning up at a restaurant. And I get to meet lots of people. The Blevinses are great—especially Ida and Emma. They come to visit me often, so I don't get lonely. And I've been sewing up a storm!"

"I can't believe you like to sew." Right now she looked like a siren, not a seamstress.

"Why?"

"You don't seem to be the type." His imagination was going wild as she wriggled beneath the towel. He could see a shoulder, then a knee, then part of one breast. And it made him want to see more. Worse yet, *to touch.*

"Sewing is my favorite hobby," she continued, oblivious to Mac's discomfort. "I haven't been able to sew because I had to sell my machine. Thank goodness, Ida left her old machine in the cabin and said I could use it anytime. I'm going to help her redecorate all the cabins."

"I'm impressed. I'll admit, I wasn't sure if it would work out."

"You were uneasy about me, weren't you?"

"No." He hesitated. "Well, yes. I didn't really know you. And the Blevinses are friends—"

"And you didn't know if you could trust me to be a good employee."

He shrugged. "I wasn't sure this would be the right job for you."

She giggled. "You don't know some of the crummy jobs I've had in my life, Mac. Compared to them, this one's a gem."

"You had a rough time with Wiley, didn't you?"

"Yeah. Not great."

"How long were you with him?"

"A little over four years."

"Why didn't you leave him sooner?"

"I'm still wondering about that." She shrugged. "You know, I don't think I figured it all out for myself until this trip. Once I did, though, I wanted out immediately. I probably could have planned it better and been a little closer to home. But then, I wouldn't have met you."

"He really held you back, you know that?" Mac took a big swallow of his beer. "You're a bright lady, Darlene. And you have a lot to offer."

"I'm so relieved to be out of that relationship. I feel like a new, free person. Do you understand what I'm saying, Mac?"

"Oh, yes. Sounds like my marriage. At least you weren't married to Wiley. And you had no real ties—no children." Mac gestured futilely and let his hand fall on his thigh.

"You have a kid?" Darlene sat upright. Maybe they had more in common than she figured.

"Not me. My former wife had one. And he was nothing but trouble between us."

Darlene frowned. She hadn't expected this from Mac.

"Normally I like kids. But this one was intent on keeping his mother for himself. And he drove me nuts. He was a spoiled brat, and she couldn't see it. We argued all the time about him—who could give him permission to go and do, who would discipline him and how. We could never agree on anything that pertained to him."

"Your former wife had custody?"

"Yeah, so he lived with us most of the time. At first I didn't mind that arrangement. I could understand a woman wanting her child living with her. After he'd been to his father's for a weekend, though, he would return like a monster for a few days. He managed to pit us against each other on every issue."

"In what ways?"

"Everything. She wanted me to live with him, but not have any disciplinary rights. She wanted me to support him, but not be able to develop any relationship. And the kid never missed an opportunity to taunt me. He was wise. He got his way. In the end, his mother and I split mainly because of differences we just couldn't work out." Mac shook his head. "And I'll never let myself get in that position again."

Darlene's heart sank. As Mac continued to talk about the miserable life he had had with his former wife and her son, Darlene knew she couldn't tell him about her own son.

Oh well, it wouldn't matter. Not really. She'd be headed back to Arkansas before too long anyway.

When her clothes were dry, Mac offered to drive her home.

"Okay." She grabbed her warm clothes and headed for the bathroom. "I'm definitely not crossing those rocks! Never again!"

Mac watched her lush figure disappear, one end of the towel flapping, one pale thigh showing. Lord, that woman did things to him! Turned him on, that's what she did! All he could think of was how to get her into his bed! And yet, he knew that he had to resist. Not that she wouldn't be great. Why, those lips of hers were made to be kissed. But he just couldn't see himself getting involved with a woman like Darlene. Besides, he knew she would leave Bear Creek as soon as she could.

Quietly they drove the short distance to the cabins. When he pulled to a stop, Mac thanked her again for the curtains.

Darlene expressed her gratitude for his rescuing her from sure drowning, then spontaneously stretched across the seat and kissed him on the cheek. It was just the impetus Mac needed. He swept his arms around her and pulled her closer. Their hot breaths mingled, and he was set afire by her warmth. Before he went up in flames, he pressed his lips to hers.

The electricity was overwhelming when they touched. Darlene had never felt so powerfully attracted to anyone as she was to Mac. She went with those feelings willingly, melting against him, thoroughly enjoying the moment.

Then, as if some warning bell had sounded, Mac pulled away from her.

Darlene scooted back into her seat. Cool air brushed her hot cheeks, sending a shiver over her.

"Darlene, I—" Mac halted with a heavy sigh and looked out the window. One arm remained loosely around her shoulders.

"If you're trying to apologize for kissing me, don't," she said tartly. "I enjoyed it too much for regrets." When his answer was nothing but uncomfortable silence, she added, "I have feelings, too, you know."

"I'm... I'm aware of that." He knotted one fist and bounced it nervously on the steering wheel. "I'm trying to resist you, Darlene. I've never been so attracted to anyone that I couldn't have. Shouldn't have."

His admission made her feel better, and her voice picked up a little lilt. "You know something funny? I'm trying hard to resist you, too, Mac." She paused, then continued: "I want you to know that I'm not eager for another man right now. I'm just coming out of a bad relationship. I'm not even sure I know what a good one is."

"Me, either." His voice was low and heavy sounding. "But I'd sure like to try... with you." He couldn't believe his own words. Did he really want this? His body was responding affirmatively. Only his logic registered resistance. He worked hard to push that resisting logic aside.

"I... would, too." She glanced at him in the semidarkness. He was looking straight ahead, his profile outlined in the shadows. Mac seemed to be the strongest, most self-assured man she'd ever known. But tonight, he'd revealed another side. Here was a man who'd made mistakes in the past and wasn't afraid to admit them. And still, he was willing to try again. Perhaps they had more in common than she'd realized.

"Would you?" he asked softly.

"Yes."

"No strings attached if it doesn't work?"

"That's the only way." She touched his hand, the one at her shoulder. Lacing her fingers with his, she squeezed lightly. "Do you want to come in?" she whispered.

His response was slow and intense as he turned to her, cupping her chin. He looked into her dark, sensual eyes. "You know I do." He lowered his head and kissed her again.

5

DARLENE FUMBLED with the door key in the dark. She had been so anxious to leave for Mac's house this afternoon that she'd forgotten to leave her porch light on. When the lock finally opened, she stumbled across the still-unfamiliar room and groped for the lamp.

She paused before switching on the light, trying to calm her racing heart. *This isn't forever. It's for now. You can always back out. Mac isn't pressuring you.*

But the lightning jolt impact of their innocent kiss wouldn't leave her. His lips had actually caressed hers, pressing so lightly that she'd wanted to forge them together with all her meager strength. And oh, how she'd felt when they touched! The warm circle of his arms made her feel safe, as if she belonged right there.

She'd only meant to give him a quick, affectionate kiss, to show her gratitude for all his help. Instead, the kiss had turned into a four-star humdinger! Unexpectedly she had been drawn into his masculinity, wanting more—much more—than that one, simple little kiss. And he had, too; she could tell from his reactions. But he had pulled back, and she had moved away—both of them pretending it hadn't happened that way. Now, there was no denying. Darlene switched on the light.

When she turned to face Mac, she knew she wouldn't stop this momentum. *She wanted Mac to make love to her.* She gazed at him for a long, appreciative moment as he stood by the door with his hands stuffed halfway into his jeans pockets, thumbs hooked on the outside. Oh, my, he was terribly appealing!

He looked completely relaxed. Only his eyes told the truth; they were passionately dark. She wondered what he was thinking—if he thought she was sexy. She almost laughed at the notion. How could jeans and a striped rugby shirt be sexy?

And yet, he was dressed no better, and he was extremely sexy to her. She'd known from the first that Mac Jackson was no ordinary man. When she gazed up at his proud face—the square chin covered with a short beard, the heavy-lidded eyes, the lips waiting for hers—Darlene felt the sharp twist of desire curl through her body. And she wanted to feel him next to her, against her, naked.

His lean, energetic body enticed her. Oh, Mac Jackson was someone special, all right. And she wasn't about to miss a spectacular moment with him. Tonight he could be hers. She grew hot all over, just thinking about the possibilities.

The space across the room that separated them seemed vast. Darlene shivered nervously and rubbed her arms. She should say something sophisticated and alluring. Why couldn't she come up with something clever? Instead, she couldn't think of a thing—except how he might look naked.

Mac gestured toward the blackened fireplace. "Could I start a fire? It's a little cool in here."

She nodded eagerly. "The wood's on the porch."

While Mac worked to kindle a blaze, Darlene turned to the kitchen. They should have something more to enhance the mood. Music. She switched on the radio and all she could get was country music. She settled for George Strait.

And wine. If she were really cool, and had the money, she would have had Chardonnay on hand. Or a six-pack of beer, at the very least. But she was neither cool nor did she have much money. So all she could offer him was . . . hot tea. She smiled, remembering her joking conversation with Ida about the very masculine Mac Jackson sitting down to a cup of tea.

She watched him, down on one knee before the fireplace. The muscles in his arms flexed when he lifted the logs. His large hands stacked them easily. She quickly decided that hot tea wouldn't bother his masculinity one bit and put on a kettle of water.

Sure enough, the fire added a welcome warmth to the room. The mood was set. The flickering yellow-gold flames cast a sensuous glow over everything, including Mac, who sat cross-legged on the large braided rug in front of the fireplace, waiting for her.

She brought two cups of tea and joined him. "I hope you like hot spiced tea." Darlene suddenly realized she knew very little about this man with whom she felt so comfortable. She didn't know his likes and dislikes, his odd quirks, his habits, his desires. . . . But she couldn't wait to learn everything about him.

"Tea sounds fine."

"Sorry I don't have a beer or—"

He placed a single finger on her lips. "Don't apologize for anything. No apologies, no regrets. Okay? You didn't know this would happen." He paused and looked at her with a teasing grin. "Or did you?"

"Of course not." She squared her shoulders. "I didn't expect this or . . . what I feel for you. It's been strange, Mac. From that first night I spent at your house, I've . . . liked you. And this . . . what we're doing tonight . . . is probably dangerous."

"You think I'm dangerous?"

His fragrance captured her senses. "I, uh . . ." How could she possibly think this mountain man was dangerous? The danger was in her own head. "Maybe it's me. From that first night, I've wanted you, Mac. Do you think I'm terrible?"

"No. You're honest. And I find that intoxicating."

Softly Mac began to stroke the planes of her face, tracing her jaw back to her ear, trailing his fingers over her cheekbone. He bent to kiss the places he had touched, letting his lips linger at her earlobe. Her fresh, clean fragrance had a familiar smell, and he knew she had used his cologne when she'd dressed in his bathroom tonight. He almost laughed aloud. That was so like Darlene—to share something of his, to take a part of him with her.

His thumb caressed her lower lip, and she opened her mouth invitingly. He buried his other hand beneath her hair, gently turning her head upward for another longed-for kiss. Their lips met, matching and sipping gingerly. Each sip created a fervor until finally he forged them together with a powerful, consuming passion.

Eventually he lifted his lips from hers. His voice was slightly hoarse. "Darlene, darlin' . . . To be honest, I've wanted you from the beginning, too. I've made a special effort to stay away from you."

"Why?"

"Because of this. I knew I couldn't stop."

She sighed and rested her head against his shoulder. "Why have we been fighting this?"

"Right now I can't think of one sensible reason." He kissed her again, murmuring between kisses, "Can't stay away... from you... any longer."

Darlene could feel her emotional sensitivity mounting with each sweetly probing kiss. She felt breathless and ravished—and she hadn't discarded a stitch of clothing! Mac's presence overwhelmed her as he drew her closer. She felt his heat radiate through her, and she longed to feel more, to have his strong body against hers.

"Oh, Darlene, you are a great adventure," he murmured as he kissed along the column of her neck.

She lifted her chin, thrilling to the soft prickle of his beard on her skin, and whispered, "You make me feel so daring." Darlene arched so that her breast brushed against his chest and her slender body curved into his.

Mac groaned softly and worked his hands beneath her sweater in back and unhooked her bra.

She gasped with pleasure as his hands slid around to the front to cup her breasts.

"No turning back." He pressed her nipples between his thumbs and forefingers. "No bailout."

"That's okay with me." She straddled his lap and hitched her hips close to him. "I like living recklessly." She shuddered as his hands gently squeezed the fullness of her breasts.

"Darlene, we're heading on a collision course." He unsnapped her jeans and slipped one hand inside to caress her buttocks.

She started unbuttoning his shirt. "Danger ahead," she announced with a laugh as she opened his shirt and began to stroke the muscular wall of his chest with her tongue. His skin quivered under her touch. She pushed the shirt down from his shoulders. "Ahh," she exclaimed admiringly.

Mac thought he would burst with anticipation as he hurriedly pulled her sweater off and kissed the generous swells of her breasts. He was overwhelmed by the urge to bury his face in them. Soon she would be all his.

When he nibbled the distended tips, Darlene moaned. She'd never felt such strong, naked desire. She wanted to take him in a mad rush.

He must have sensed her longing. Or else his own need took control. There was no more playing around, no more waiting. With feverish, fast-moving hands, Mac began to tear off her remaining clothes, but Darlene took over, pulling her legs out of her jeans and tossing them aside. Then she unsnapped his and slid the zipper down, before returning to explore the broad expanse of his bare chest. She relished the feel of the curly mat of brown hair and the rippling muscles beneath her fingertips. After bending to kiss his lips, she moved lower to tease his beadlike nipples with her tongue. Relentlessly she tasted and suckled.

He grabbed her hands and kissed her fingers. His voice was hoarse, his breath hot on her hands. "Darlin', we haven't discussed birth control. I didn't come prepared. I didn't expect—"

"That's taken care of," she told him with a little smile, glad that she had done something right for once in her life. "I'm still on the Pill."

"Then there's no worry? I wouldn't want to—"

She lowered her eyes, thinking how her world had changed twelve years ago because neither she nor her young lover had been so carefully responsible. That was the night she had gotten pregnant. "Not a worry in the world," she said confidently. "We'll be all right."

"Good." With a low, sexy laugh, he leaned back on the braided rug, pulling her across his chest. "Come here, my darlin' Darlene. This is where you belong. With me."

"Seems that way, doesn't it?" She framed his face with her hands and smiled as she presented him with a series of kisses.

He put his hands on her hips and aligned their bodies to touch intimately. *Oh, yes, indeed,* she agreed silently. This was exactly where she belonged. Where he belonged, too.

Mac was boldly, excitingly aroused beneath her. She moved her thighs alongside his and nestled her breasts against him, molding their softness to the muscular firmness of his chest. The crisp, masculine curls teased her skin as she undulated over him sensually. It was obvious that she was enjoying herself.

"I want you, Darlene. I've wanted you since that first night you stayed in my house."

"I find that hard to believe, Mac. I looked pretty bad that night."

"Like a well-worn rag doll," he agreed. "But I knew that underneath was a beautiful lady with delicate skin and wonderful eyes—a lady I wanted to know better." He caressed her fanny with both hands, then ran them up her back. "Someone to know completely. A lady to love."

"Oh, Mac..." No one had ever called her that. There'd been other names, but "lady" was not one of them. And "beautiful" was a term usually reserved for others. In his own special way, Mac gave her dignity.

She rested her head on the cushion of hair on his chest, taking sensual pleasure in every place their bodies touched. "You make me feel so good, Mac. This is exactly where I've wanted to be—touching you, loving you."

Mac stroked her back, his large, strong hands caressing every silken inch of her. He slipped one hand between them. Her skin was so creamy smooth and inviting. She quivered and moaned softly when he found the velvety warmth of her femininity. He wanted her intensely—oh, how he ached to sink into her satiny comfort, gratifying his immediate needs! But he had to make sure he took her with him. This time, this important first time, it had to be good. Better than good—it had to be perfect.

Darlene caressed his lips with hers, pressing kisses randomly over his face. Her body moved freely over his, setting him on fire. He was hard and rugged and she loved feeling him like this. She knew what she was doing to him, knew she was driving him crazy. The knowledge spurred her on.

He trembled, trying to wait, trying to resist the urge to take her completely...fast...hard. He wanted to plunge into her with all his strength. Circling the warm curves of her bottom, Mac molded his male hardness to her feminine pliancy. His longing for her mounted with each heated movement, each fiery breath.

Darlene's body responded to him in every way. She could feel the unmistakable electricity of his desire surging through her as their bodies intertwined. He was the sexiest man she'd ever known, and she marveled at his loving patience. Their hot-skinned coupling re-awakened yearnings she thought she'd abandoned long ago. Rolling her hips forward, she slowly and purposefully showed him what she wanted. The motion drove them both to the brink.

With fervent passion, he captured her lips with his as he turned her, hovering briefly before taking her with his entire body. Whispering softly in her ear, he sought the magnificent silk between her thighs.

The only noise in the night was the crackle of the fire. Suddenly the well-stacked logs shifted, sending up a shower of sparks. In that moment, their union became complete.

Darlene soared. Her spirits rose along with her response to the man she had secretly desired.

Lying in Mac's arms, she felt warm and secure and completely relaxed. "Yes. Oh, yes," she murmured, stroking his side. "It was better than I dared to dream."

"Hmm," he mumbled in agreement, nuzzling her neck.

"The best," she stated simply. "The very best." Feeling happy and content for the first time in years, she smiled, then dozed in his arms.

Her dreams of a real man who was secure in himself and who cared for her had been fulfilled tonight. But was it possible for her to find love? No. She'd convinced herself long ago that love was something others had—not her. *Love* was reserved strictly for Darlene's dreams.

She woke minutes—or was it hours?—later when he lifted her to the bed. The sheets were cool. His body was warm. And when they made love again, they proceeded slowly and leisurely. Even in the heat of passion Darlene was aware of deeper feelings for him, of something greater than the desire that had drawn them together. But she couldn't be sure. She'd never experienced anything like this before.

With the earliest light of daybreak filtering through the trees surrounding the cabin, Mac stirred. Quietly he rose from the bed and began to do what he knew he must.

Half awake, Darlene turned over and raised her head. "Mac? Where're you going?"

"Home."

"Why?"

"I... I just... should."

"You don't want anyone to see your Jeep here, do you?"

"To be honest, it wouldn't look very good for you."

She leaned her head back and laughed heartily. "Nobody's ever tried to protect *my* reputation before. This is a real first."

He gave her a rueful look and picked up his jeans from the floor where he'd dropped them. "You're starting fresh here, Darlene. It's something that will be important if you decide to stick around awhile."

She turned over and propped herself up on her elbows. "You know something, Mac? I don't care how it looks. Last night was so good, so...wonderful. Nearly perfect, I'd say."

"Perfect?" He chuckled. "That's a pretty high rating for the first time. Now, how do we top that?"

"We'll just have to keep trying," she responded with a sassy grin.

Half dressed, he came to her. He wrapped her in his big embrace, covers and all. "Now, that will be a distinct pleasure that'll keep me coming back again and again. But right now, I do have to go. Trust me. It's for the best." He kissed her gently.

She folded her hands beneath her head and watched him with sleepy delight. "Mac, what are you doing here? I mean, what are you doing way out here?"

He shrugged and started putting on his socks and shoes. "Living a quiet, modest life."

"But why here?"

"It's a good place to stay out of the way and out of trouble."

"You? In trouble?" It sounded preposterous to Darlene. Mac seemed so perfectly steady and downright decent.

"Sure. I've had my share. And I just decided that I wanted to escape it all." He stood and looked around for his shirt. "I just wanted to start someplace new."

"After your divorce?"

Rescuing his shirt from the other side of the fireplace, he walked toward her as he put it on. "Yeah. After the disaster of my divorce *and* the devastation of losing my job. I figured I had nothing more to lose. So

I moved here and started new again. The one thing I had going for me was experience."

"Losing your job?" She frowned and sat up, pulling the covers around her shoulders. Darlene couldn't imagine Mac being fired. "What job? How did that happen?" She thought that kind of thing only happened to someone like Wiley; not someone nice like Mac.

"Oh, I got myself into a world of trouble up in Kentucky." He stood beside the bed stuffing his shirttail into his jeans.

Bewitched by his every movement, Darlene watched his hands and remembered their lovemaking. When he finished dressing, he sat beside her on the bed and propped his hands on either side of her head. "I'll tell you about it sometime."

"Tell me now."

He shook his head, then lowered it for a quick kiss. "Maybe when we have more time, and it seems important. As for right now, it's too early for you to get up, so go back to sleep. Pretend I'm there beside you."

"I wish." She hated to see him go. Being with Mac was so natural, so comfortable.

He kissed her forehead, her nose, then her lips. "You're beautiful." He caressed her tousled hair. "I'll be back."

"Today?"

"Not today. Maybe tomorrow."

With regret, she watched him leave the room, knowing he was right. He couldn't stay. They both had separate lives. And neither wanted a tangled involvement. Maybe it was best this way—to have him come occasionally; no apologies, no regrets.

Eventually, as he'd advised, she dozed. In her dreams, Mac Jackson loved her in his own perfect way. And, in return, she loved him.

But when she woke again a few hours later, reality set in and Darlene began to think about what she'd done. In a weak moment of undenied passion, she had begun a relationship with a man who would probably be horrified at the knowledge that she had a son. Not only that, but she felt sure that Mac would walk away from her in a minute if he knew. So, did she have any regrets?

Her thoughts wandered to memories of their love-making, and subconsciously she smiled. The whole experience had been great. No, there were no real regrets. It was definitely better to have loved Mac once than never to have loved him at all.

Her mood changed, however, when she recalled how angry he'd been last night as he related his experiences with his former wife and her demanding young son. Darlene didn't want to lose Mac at this point. Therefore, her conclusion was simple. There was only one way to handle it.

She wouldn't tell Mac about her son, Ken. That was all.

LATER THAT DAY, Ida came by to take Darlene shopping.

Darlene swung open the door. "Come on in. I'll be ready in a jiff." She went back to her makeup at the bathroom mirror but left the door open so they could talk.

"Hey, he's cute," Ida said, walking directly to Darlene's bed.

Darlene looked up quickly. The only "he" who had been in her bed was Mac. Could Ida tell she'd had a lover last night? She'd been very careful to remove all traces of Mac. She'd made the bed and washed and put away their teacups. What if Ida should find out? Would she care? Would Mac? Darlene definitely had got the idea that he wanted their liaison kept secret. She relaxed when she saw Ida reach for the doll on her bed.

"I wouldn't have thought to turn this little one into a boy, but with a baseball cap and jeans, he's perfect!" Ida exclaimed, inspecting the doll. "And I like the way you made his face with just those big eyes. Leaves lots to your imagination."

Darlene applied a light coat of lipstick. She had liked the way the doll had turned out, too. He reminded her in some ways of Ken—always in jeans and a sweatshirt and scuffed tennis shoes. "Hope you don't mind that I fixed him up. He seemed to need something."

"Course not. I wanted you to. I'm glad to see that you're interested enough in dolls to work on this one."

Darlene tossed her head as she brushed her hair. "It was the funniest thing. He seemed to demand my attention to finish him."

"Oh, yes, they do that," Ida agreed with a chuckle. "They have a strange power."

"Power?" Darlene questioned. "Well, I don't know about that, but . . . it was strange. I couldn't stop until he was finished."

"It's hard to explain, but they do have personalities. You'll see." Holding the newly made doll at arm's length, she scrutinized him with narrowed eyes. "What's his name?"

"Name? Oh, I don't know." Darlene carefully applied a thin coat of mascara to her already dark lashes.

"Does he have a personality?" Ida asked with a sly grin.

"Not much." Darlene shrugged. "He's just a kid."

"Doesn't he remind you of someone?"

A slow smile spread across Darlene's face, and she turned to Ida. Her eyes sparkled. "He sort of reminds me of a kid back in Arkansas named Ken," she replied softly.

"Then, let's call him Ken. That's a good name for him." Ida placed the doll back on the bed, leaving him propped on a pillow as if he could watch what was happening in the room.

"No, I—" Darlene started, then gazed at the doll for a second. She couldn't name a doll after her own son. *Could she?* The face seemed to grin at her, but that was strictly her imagination, for all he had to form his facial expression were big, button eyes. No nose or mouth. He seemed receptive to the name. "Okay," she agreed slowly. "Ken, he is."

"And who is this Ken?"

Without thinking it through, Darlene answered, "My son."

The room was dead silent, and Darlene realized her mistake. What she had revealed to Ida had a good chance of getting to Mac. And she definitely didn't want Mac to know.

"You have a son, Darlene?"

"He, uh, lives with my brother in Arkansas. It . . . happened a long time ago and I'd appreciate it if you'd just keep it our secret."

"Of course, honey," Ida murmured sympathetically. "I won't tell a soul."

Darlene gave her hair another vigorous brushing, then entered the room with a quickly formed smile. "Okay. Ready to go?"

Ida nodded and dangled the car keys. "Would you like to drive?"

"Me?"

"You do have a license, don't you?"

"Sure. I have a valid license in Arkansas and Missouri. Is that good enough?" Darlene looked at Ida curiously. "You don't drive?"

"Oh, I *can*. I just don't like to very much. It makes me nervous. Whenever I can get someone else to do the driving, I take advantage."

Darlene took the keys and slipped her arm around Ida's shoulder. "Well, I'll be glad to be the designated driver."

"Do you have the measurements?"

Darlene patted her purse. "I measured every window in cabin three today. And I made a list of hardware I need for the repairs."

Their first stop in town was the fabric shop. As they studied various bolts of material, Darlene asked, "What kind of fabric do you have in mind?"

"I don't know. Something country, like the other cabins, I guess. Maybe red-and-white checks."

"Why does it have to be like the others? Why not make it something different?"

"Like what?"

Darlene lifted a piece imprinted with bears. "Make it a hunter's cabin. Decorate it with bearskin rugs and deer antlers on the walls."

Ida's face lit up. "Boyd has an old deer rack at the house that I've been trying to get rid of for years. And we have an old rug made from a bear Boyd's daddy killed many years ago. I've always hated that thing, but I'll bet it would look good on the cabin floor. We could decorate the hunter's lodge with leftovers in our garage. That's a great idea."

"It is?" Darlene lifted her head. It was the first time she had put forth an idea for anything that wasn't rejected by Wiley or her family.

Ida clasped her hands as her enthusiasm mounted. "We'll do it up right and send out some advertising."

"I'll bet folks would love to stay in a cabin decorated for hunters." Darlene glanced at Ida and winked. "And we can fix the next one up for fishermen." Fishermen like Mac were more her style, anyway.

They spent the next few hours shopping for everything on Darlene's list. Finally, arms loaded with purchases, they headed for the car. While waiting for the light to change, Darlene noticed a sign in the window of the corner building. It advertised typing classes every Monday night. Typing! She could learn to type by coming to a class for six weeks! It sounded too good to be true. She read the sign again and made a mental note to call the school doing the advertising.

The light changed, and Ida started across the street, chatting enthusiastically about the new project. "The bottom line is that I'm sure it'll bring more customers. And Boyd should be happy about that."

"You don't think he'll object to the decorating idea, do you?"

"Not if we show him how we can bring in more customers and make more money."

On the way home, Ida continued to talk about the new decorating project for the cabin, but Darlene's mind was on other things. She imagined typing letters to Ken and even surprising Mac with her new typing skills. Wouldn't that be fun?

Abruptly, Ida interrupted her thoughts. "Darlene! Are you listening to me?"

"Yes— Uh, actually, no, Ida. I was thinking about something else."

"What's so all-fired important that it's completely occupying your mind?"

"Oh, I saw a sign back in town advertising teaching a certain class that I'd like to take."

"And what is it?"

"Typing."

"Typing? Why do you want to learn that? You use the H 'n' P system just fine."

"But I don't like the H 'n' P system, Ida. I want to know the keyboard." She shrugged. "It's just a personal challenge."

Ida looked closely at Darlene. "You like challenges, don't you?"

"It seems that my whole life has been a challenge, Ida. Nothing has worked out easily for me." She gestured.

"So I have to go after everything, or I'll be swept away, always doing what someone else wants instead of what *I* want."

"That's pretty smart of you to realize that. I've never thought much about it. Just did what needed to be done next." Ida shook her head. "I guess that's why I'm still trying to 'find myself,' as the kids say."

"I'd say you have your hands full, taking care of Byron and Emma."

"Yes, I do. But I want more. Something for me, like you said. Something that I like to do."

"I understand completely. Besides going back home to Arkansas, what I want right now is to learn to type without looking at the keyboard."

"Takes practice," Ida said.

"That class can teach me how. I just have to figure out how to get there every Monday night."

"Well, that's no problem. Just take my car."

"Oh, no, I couldn't do that, Ida."

"And why not?"

"Just because—" She paused. "What would Boyd say?"

"Who cares what Boyd says? It's my car. And you're my friend. If I want to let you borrow my car, I can. So it's settled. You sign up for that class and take my car."

Darlene turned onto The Bear Creek road. She was going to learn to type! "Thank you, Ida."

When she pulled to a stop at Ida's house, Ida hesitated. "I know this is none of my business, but have you seen Mac lately?"

"Why, yes, Ida. Just last night." Darlene tried to sound casual, but her throat got tight when she talked about Mac. She figured if she denied seeing him, that would stir up more inquiries. And she couldn't lie. "I, uh, went over to his place to take him the curtains I made for him."

"You made him curtains?" Ida's face lit up. "What did he say about that?"

"He was surprised that I could sew. And he thought they would look fine in his kitchen." Darlene grabbed her packages and insisted that she had to hurry home. Before Ida could press her further about Mac, she was gone.

Darlene was not prepared to tell her about Mac spending the night. Not just yet. Anyway, she'd already revealed more than she should when she told Ida about Ken.

6

MAC HAD BEEN KEEPING Darlene company while she worked on the decorating project for the third cabin. When the curtains were finished, he even helped her hang them. In the past, such a domestic task would have been something he would have avoided at all costs. Yet, it still seemed perfectly natural doing anything with Darlene.

Their relationship amazed and delighted him. What had begun as undeniable passion soon developed into something...more. Although he and Darlene were spending more and more time together, they were unwilling to admit it or even discuss the reasons why.

"How's this?" Mac asked as he stood on a step stool, hanging another set of curtains.

Darlene narrowed her eyes and framed the window with her thumbs and hands. "Up a little to the left."

Mac stretched. "Okay?"

"Umm... Move a little to the right."

Mac juggled his footing on the step stool. "How's this?"

"Umm... Maybe a little—"

"Come on, Darlene!"

"Okay! Hold it right there! It's perfect!" She grabbed a nail and climbed onto the stool beside him. Wriggling her hips next to his, she said, "You're doing a great job, Mac. Now, hold still while I mark both sides."

"How can I hold still when you're so temp—" He took a groaning breath. "Just make it snappy."

"I am." She leaned gently against Mac who stood spread-eagled, holding up the curtains and rod against the wall. "You're doing great. I don't know how I'd manage without your help, Mac."

He breathed deeply as her body caressed his. "I don't know how I've managed to stay away from you all this time while we held material up to the windows." He kissed her earlobe, murmuring sexy words into her ear. "We can close the curtains and..."

"Now, now," she admonished with a teasing smile. "We have a job to do here. No time for messing around."

"When can we mess around?" he challenged with a boyish grin.

"We have the upstairs windows yet to do."

He groaned audibly, but gamely installed the hooks for the curtain rods, then followed her upstairs. "Ahh, the bedroom. My favorite area," he said, warming to the surroundings. "Hey, I like this. A fireplace, a bear rug, and thou."

"The rug belonged to Boyd's father. It's in keeping with the new theme for the cabin."

"Theme? Bears?"

"Fun-ny. We're going to name this cabin Crockett, after the famous Tennessean, Davy Crockett. Didn't he kill a bear or something?"

Mac nodded. "He was also a congressman. And he got himself into that fiasco at the Alamo in Texas."

"Well, he was a hunter, too. And that's the theme of this cabin," Darlene explained as she pushed the gathered curtains onto the rod. She gestured at the painting of hunters and their dogs hanging above the mantel. "I'm going to suggest that we decorate cabin four in a fisherman's theme. You know—with rods and reels and wicker creels."

"I like that idea."

"We could have a Cherokee Indian-motif cabin, and an Opry-star cabin and decorate it with music and pictures of country-music stars."

"You're just full of ideas."

"Sometimes my mind just shifts into overdrive." She dodged his teasing pinch. "For this cabin, we're looking for a coonskin cap and any kind of hunting paraphernalia. You wouldn't happen to have anything lying around gathering dust, would you?"

"I have an old powder-horn. Could you use that?"

"Why, that sounds great. Where did you get it?"

"It was in some of the stuff that I inherited from my father. I think it belonged to his grandfather. Also, there's a turkey caller."

"What's that?"

"It's a hollowed-out box carved from wood with a separate top-piece. Both sections are coated with chalk and when rubbed together, they make a turkey sound. Then, supposedly, those turkeys come running."

"If they belonged to your dad, would you be willing to contribute them to the Blevinses' cabins?" She handed him the curtains gathered on the rod and pointed to the window. "Hold these up there, please."

"Sure. I have no use for them." He climbed onto the step stool again and lifted the curtains up for her inspection. "This was all your idea, wasn't it?"

"Redecorating? No. Ida wanted it done."

"I'm talking about fixing the cabins with a theme. That's a very good idea, especially the fishing one."

"I just thought it would be neat to have the cabins different, that's all." She shrugged. "Move over to the left a little."

"Admit it, Darlene—" he struggled to keep his balance as he moved according to her directions "—you have some very good ideas."

She waved off his compliment. "This is the first time I've ever had *any* ideas."

"I can't believe that."

"It's true. Almost everything I've ever done has been initiated by someone else."

"Except stopping in Gatlinburg."

"Right." She smiled up at him. "Best idea I've had yet."

"Except for stopping smoking. You have stopped, haven't you?"

She raised her right hand. "Haven't had a puff in eight days."

"Good girl."

Wiggling her hands wildly in the air, she started dancing around crazily. "Eight days, twelve hours, twenty minutes and thirty-three seconds! And I'm not craving anything. I've just eaten twelve tons of Life Savers and chewed a million sticks of gum!"

He hooted with laughter. She was such a welcome addition to his life, it was worth all the domestic chores she asked him to do for her.

When the curtains looked exactly the way she wanted them, Mac hopped down and took her in his arms. "You going to win this smoking bet?"

"You're darned right!"

"I'm proud of you." He kissed her nose and lips, then tumbled her onto the bed. "I have a great idea," he mumbled into her ear. "How about if we christened the new cabin for hunters?"

"How original!" She giggled, trying to escape the tickling of his lips and the soft bristles of his beard. "You have only one idea, Mac. Only the location varies."

"Not so!" He nuzzled her neck. "But you've gotta admit, christening sounds like fun!"

"What if somebody came up here—like Ida?"

"She won't come out here today. Her sewing club meets today." He kissed her lips, letting his tongue tease the corners until she felt desire all the way to her toes. "We're all alone, darlin'. Just you and me. Why not make love in the hunter's cabin? Give me three good reasons why not?"

"Three? I can't think," she murmured breathlessly, responding to his sweet, soft kisses. "Not with you...doing that." When he kissed her, she became weak-kneed.

"Doing what?" He continued to tease her with his persistent kisses.

"Oh, you *are* a slick-tongued devil." She laughed huskily and writhed in his embrace as he placed kisses along the length of her neck.

"And you, my lil' darlin', are one sexy lady. I feel I know you well. We've grown so close, after all, we've made love."

She smiled at him sadly. "I had such a different life before I came to Gatlinburg—and met you."

He shrugged. "So did I."

"No. You're so . . . steady and established. And you have your businesses. Why, I didn't even—" She halted. Would she spoil their fun? Ruin their relationship with her admission? But she had to be honest with Mac. He *didn't* know her very well, didn't know all the big mistakes of her life, all the skeletons in her personal closet. And it wasn't quite fair. He should know some things . . . maybe not *all* things.

"Didn't even what?"

She took a deep breath. "You might feel differently about me if you knew that I didn't graduate from high school."

He frowned. So that's why she was constantly doubting herself and fighting back with her brashness. "Darlin', graduating isn't everything."

"It's proof of your accomplishments," she countered stoutly. "It means you can stick with something and see it through to the end. And I couldn't."

"When you can't, it doesn't mean anything. Doesn't mean that you're stupid. I'm sure you had your reason."

"I did. But now it's unfinished business."

"Unfinished business can always be finished, you know."

"I'd like to do that," she said sincerely. "I'd really like that."

"Then I think you should."

"Do you . . . do you think I could?"

There was her self-doubt again. "You mean, do I think you're smart enough?" He touched her face tenderly, stroking her cheek with one finger. "Of course you are, Darlene. There's no problem."

"There are plenty of problems, Mac. But you give me such confidence, I think I can do anything."

"No, darlin'. You arrived on the scene with that bold confidence. Right up here." He tapped her head, then bent to kiss her fervently.

Darlene felt ten feet tall. She submitted to her feelings, her marvelous trust in the man whose arms were wrapped around her. When she was with him—whether making love or hanging curtains—she felt his respect and his caring for her. She hoped it never changed. Yet a part of her knew that it couldn't last forever. Someday she would leave the mountains—and Mac. But for now, he was hers. And so she opened her arms and her heart to him.

With murmured words of affection and a fervor they couldn't halt—and didn't even try to—they christened the hunter's cabin. It gave them another shared secret, another bond.

THE NEXT WEEK, as clouds hung heavily above them, Mac and Darlene were heading up the Bear Creek trail.

"Who would plan a picnic on a rainy day?"

"It isn't raining yet."

"See those clouds?"

Darlene looked up and frowned. But she continued without hesitation, lugging the prized picnic basket.

She was usually too busy to try to reach Mac's heart with her good cooking. But today, she had taken the time and baked a chocolate cake for him. And it was going to be fabulous. She could hardly wait to see his face when he bit into it. "If you thought it would rain, why did you bring your fishing rod?"

"Just in case. I want to try my new lures." They hiked awhile in silence, then Mac motioned to her. "Here. There's a good fishing hole where there's a granddaddy trout that eludes everyone. Let me see if I can tempt him."

Darlene sat on a rock and dropped the basket on the ground between her legs, grateful for the rest. It was the perfect time for a cigarette. But she pushed that thought out of her mind and turned her attention to Mac.

He headed for the stream with the eagerness of a kid with a new toy. They'd been hiking up Bear Creek for a good hour. Even though rain had threatened to ruin their day, she was determined to stick to their plan. What was a little rain, anyway?

Mondays and Tuesdays were light workdays for both of them, and they often spent those days or evenings together. By Wednesday, a few guests would start to arrive. The bulk of the visitors came on Thursdays and Fridays. And the weekend was always busy, as Darlene had to be available to accommodate her guests and Mac had fishing tours lined up. Any time they spent together was usually squeezed in late at night. That added to the intrigue of their relationship, and it made days like this one more special.

Mac turned and nodded for her to come closer. Silently she moved to his side. As she stood beside Mac, his strength seemed to reach out and embrace her, and Darlene felt stronger and more secure near him.

He curled one arm around her and pointed across the large pool that was damned naturally by several large rocks. "See that whopper rainbow trout . . . he's playing hard to get," he said in a whisper.

Darlene strained to catch the shape of the fish beneath the rippling surface of the water. "I see him!" she returned in a low voice. "Let me try."

Mac handed her the rod. "Just hold it like this. Left hand here, thumb here. Aim the tip. Don't let out too much line. It'll get hooked in the trees."

Darlene glanced at him as he gave her a quick lesson in fly-casting. She held the rod, aimed carefully and flicked her wrist. The line doubled gracefully over the water as the lure landed near the rock where she'd seen the fish. Her aim wasn't quite as accurate as Mac's, but she obviously wasn't a novice at the skill, either.

"Pretty good for a first-timer," he drawled softly.

"Who said it was my first time?" She grinned. "I'm just rusty."

He nodded and stuffed his hands in his back pockets. "Rusty, huh? Not too bad for rusty."

"Didn't I tell you that I grew up with fishermen in my family? My pa and my brother taught me."

"Every time we're together, I find out something new and intriguing about you."

"I wouldn't call this information intriguing. We were dirt-poor and fished to put food on the table. We didn't fly-fish often. Usually we fished for large or small-mouth bass or river trout." She slowly reeled the line in and cast again. "My brother, Chase, still lives there.

He runs a fishing village at the old homeplace, if you could call it that."

"He taught you well." Mac pointed to another spot in the water. "Aim for that area."

She did as he said, pursuing the trout with diligence. They were surrounded with absolute and beautiful silence. Only the whining sounds of spring water-bugs and the occasional plop of the lure breaking the water's surface could be heard. Raindrops started to ping softly against the leaves, which acted as a multitude of tiny green umbrellas, protecting Mac and Darlene.

Suddenly a snorting noise penetrated their quiet world.

Darlene looked at Mac. "What's that?"

"Shh. Sounds like...bear." He glanced around, trying to spot the creature. "Don't move."

But Darlene knew immediately where the bear was. The picnic basket! Her fabulous chocolate cake! She wasn't about to stand there and let him ruin it. Nothing was going to spoil their fun. Before Mac could stop her, she thrust the fishing rod into his hands and darted through the trees. There, in the clearing beside the trail, tearing into the basket that she had prepared with such love, was a small, stocky black bear.

"Our tuna sandwiches! Leave that cake alone!" she screeched. "Get away!"

The bear grunted and looked up from his task. The top of the basket had been torn off and dangled from one clawed foot.

Before she could reach the clearing, something hit Darlene from behind, flattening her to the ground. Breath whooshed out of her lungs, and it took her a few seconds to realize that Mac was responsible and now lay atop her.

"Be still," he hissed into her ear.

The bear tossed the basket into the air and clumsily grabbed the sandwiches. Stuffing them into his mouth, he fumbled for the cake. That was even better and he gobbled it, letting the wrapping paper and various pieces of fruit scatter about. Then, as Darlene and Mac watched in amazement, the bear shuffled away. His wild smell lingered in the air long after he had disappeared.

Mac breathed a sigh of relief, but he remained perfectly still for a long time. It was raining harder than ever when he figured it was finally safe and helped Darlene to her feet. "You okay?" He bent to brush her jeans.

"You big oaf, you nearly killed me!" she wailed. "Why did you stop me? Look at the mess! And our lunch—"

"A bear isn't something to mess around with, Darlene. They can be very dangerous. What if he'd spotted you? And decided he'd rather bat you around than that basket?"

"I thought he'd run when he heard me."

"Usually they avoid contact with humans. But you never know. They're unpredictable. Kind of like you." He tweaked her nose, which was now wet from the rain. "What made you charge out here like that?"

"I knew he was after our cake."

"Please don't ever do that again. Bears are damned dangerous. You stay out of their sight from now on.

This one must have been hungry and was looking for food."

"Lucky for me they're vegetarians." Rain was hitting her face hard now. "I've never been so close to a bear before. He stinks!"

Mac took her arm and slowly they approached the clearing. Picnic items were scattered everywhere. The basket was ripped beyond repair. Darlene stooped and began gathering the litter. "Is he gone?"

"I'm sure he is. For now." Mac helped her clean up the mess, then retrieved his fishing rod. "Ready to go back?"

Darlene stood on the trail, rain streaming down her cheeks, her drenched hair hanging in limp strands. She propped her hands on her hips. "Well, you did it again."

"What?" Mac looked at her. Raindrops dripped from the end of his nose. His hair had parted in the middle and was plastered to his head. His beard glistened with silvery droplets.

"Rescued me." She came to him and slipped her arms around his waist. "And I want to thank you." She stood on tiptoe and kissed him while the rain pelted them harder, as if testing the quality of their endurance. The kiss continued.

Finally he lifted his head. "I didn't rescue you. I just kept you quiet for a few minutes. That, in itself, was a heroic feat."

"Why, you—" Laughing, she grabbed at his nose.

Mac dodged her attack and clamped her arms to her sides with his bear hug. "You crazy lady. Don't you see what you did was dangerous? I just wanted to keep you safe." He held her close to him, kissing her eyelids and cheeks and lips. He didn't want to think of her getting hurt. It was too horrifying. She was too important to him.

"But Mac, if he'd attacked us, he would have mauled you because you were on top." She squeezed her wet body against him and could feel the cold water from their clothes trickling down her middle. "I don't know what I would have done if you'd been hurt."

"Somehow, you would have rescued me." He kissed her again. "I have faith in you, Darlene."

"Mac—" she molded to him, melting in his arms "—you're the best...." The kiss lasted until both were completely soaked.

He touched her hair. Mac knew how he felt at this moment. And he knew those kinds of thoughts were dangerous. They led to involvement and commitment, and he'd sworn off both long ago. He didn't want to like Darlene so much, didn't want to care for her so deeply, didn't want to respond to her. But, Lord help him, he did. And he couldn't hide it any longer. "Think we'd better go, Darlene?"

"Yeah." She smiled up at him. Her vision was clouded by the rain. "Before we get wet."

Shrieking and laughing, they dashed down the path, covering the same distance in half the time. They arrived at Mac's house breathless and soggy all the way to their socks. Leaving their clothes outside the back door in a heap, they scooted inside, bare and giggling.

"Shower?"

"Yes!" She shivered. "I'm freezing!"

"This will get you warm. Guaranteed!" He pulled her into the shower with him.

Refreshing, hot water pelted their chilled bodies. Darlene lifted her face for a kiss. As their wet lips met and forged, water streamed over their closed eyes and cheeks and down their chins. Small puddles formed between them where her plump breasts met the muscular barrier of his chest.

His soapy hands slid smoothly over her silken skin. He stroked her back, tracing its gentle curve. His hands cupped her fanny, and he marveled at the way they fit together just right. Everything about her seemed to fit him—her marvelous body, her positive personality, her remarkable, unquenchable spirit.

A twist of desire tore through him when she pushed her velvety breasts against his chest. He kissed her, wanting her more than he'd wanted anyone.

No words were necessary, for each movement elicited a response. When Mac touched her, passion spiraled through her, compelling her to seek the culmination that would satisfy her longing.

They shifted positions. Firm thighs slid against each other. His hands circled her waist, then slipped upward. Her breasts filled his hands, and he bent to kiss their sweet, moist tips.

With her open hands she cupped his tight buttocks. Leaning back slightly, she arched her back and molded her body into his, enjoying the full impact of his intimacy. His arousal was bold and strong against her. Every touch was heaven.

One of his hands slid around her body, moving her closer. His other hand stroked the sensitive areas at the base of her spine. She gave a low moan, and boldly looped one leg around his thigh.

He knew, as he touched her intimately, that he was losing control. "Darlene—"

"Take me, Mac."

"Here?" Bracing his legs, he lifted her easily against him.

"Yes!" she muttered in a hiss, wrapping her legs around his hips. She arched and moaned again as he complied with her fervent, insistent demands, lowering her carefully until they merged.

She placed her hands on his shoulders and gazed down into his strong face. His blue eyes were dark as charcoal, his lips partially open allowing for heavy intakes of air. Hard and hot, he filled her, and she knew pleasure beyond anything she'd ever imagined.

He looked up, watching her reactions, gratified by her responses. Her wet hair fell forward around her face. Her beautiful brown eyes were heavy-lidded. And she was smiling. "Oh, yes . . ."

With an instinct completely beyond his control, he thrust forward.

So that he wouldn't lose his grip, he pressed her back against the tiled wall. She arched and moved with him. Faster. Harder. Deeper. Luckily they climaxed just as the shower ran out of hot water.

He wrapped her in a thick, soft towel and carried her to the bed. She snuggled into his arms. "Hold me, Mac."

"Forever," he declared, not fully realizing what he was saying. He only knew he wanted to hold her forever. And, for the first time since they'd met and made love, he was afraid she would leave.

Even in his sex-muddled mind, Mac realized that he was feeling more exhilaration in loving Darlene than he'd experienced in years. And in some ways it scared him, because now, he knew that he didn't want to lose her.

After a while, they remembered they hadn't had lunch and were hungry. Mac fixed trout on the grill with a special lemon sauce. Wearing Mac's oversize clothes while hers dried, Darlene fixed a salad and hush puppies—traditional deep-fried corn bread—to go with the fish.

He drove her home late that night. As they sat in the Jeep, prolonging the inevitable parting, she said, "It was a perfectly beautiful day, Mac."

He chuckled. "Seems like every time we're together is nearly perfect."

"Except that damn bear ruined my picnic," she added with a pout. "And my chocolate cake. Never mind. I'll bake you another one."

"Must be great. The bear sure liked it. You're pretty good with a fly rod, you know?"

"I've spent my life around fishing." She shrugged. "It comes almost naturally."

"You know, I—" Mac halted and looked at her for a minute.

"What?"

"Well, there is something you can do to help me out, if you wouldn't mind."

"Anything, Mac. I'd do anything for you."

"Next weekend I have a conflict. I've agreed to do some bookkeeping for a local trade school. It just changed management and everything's a mess. The new owner is going to be in town next weekend and wants to go over the books with me. But I have a fishing tour scheduled. This new accounting job will be much more lucrative for me than one fishing tour, so I'm considering canceling it. But I hate to, because these people have planned on it."

"I could do it."

"After seeing you with that fly rod, I believe you could. It's simple. I want as many people as possible on the tour to catch a trout." His arm slid around her shoulder. "Just make sure you stay away from any bears that might appear. And don't fall in the stream."

She framed his bearded face with her hands. "It would be pretty dangerous without you there to rescue me."

"Who's going to rescue me?" He bent to kiss her, then paused. "From you?" Their lips merged and the kiss deepened and lasted an eternity, blocking out reality. "Hmm, dangerous . . ."

"Either let me go or come in with me," she threatened.

"Can't. I have to go. You have work tomorrow. So do I."

"Right. See you...soon." She slipped out of his Jeep and ran up the back steps. When she'd unlocked the door and waved goodbye, he drove away. Slipping inside, Darlene went about getting ready for bed. She brushed her teeth, thinking how wonderfully Mac kissed her.

She changed into a gown, recalling how marvelously her body responded to his. She moved the doll named Ken and turned the covers down. Sliding into bed, Darlene reveled in the completely satisfying passion they shared. All in all, each time spent with Mac was wonderful. And getting better. They were so thoroughly compatible, so completely matched. They just seemed to go together perfectly.

And yet, there was something that kept Darlene awake; something that haunted her more each day. The more she cared for Mac, the more it troubled her that she wasn't being entirely truthful with him. What would he say if he knew she had a son? Only Mac could give her the answer. And Darlene feared that his answer would be one she didn't want to hear—one that would ruin the beauty of what they shared.

7

THE NEXT FEW WEEKS were busy for Darlene. She'd discovered that being busy helped battle the strong urge to smoke more than anything else. She finished decorating cabin three, which was renamed The Crockett, and began renting it right away. Since that quickly increased Bear Creek Cabins' revenues, it made Boyd very happy with Darlene's work. He was ready to let her redecorate all the cabins.

She took Mac's fishing group on a successful tour the next weekend, which pleased him very much. Most exciting, though, she and Ida started a new and surprisingly rewarding hobby.

"How's the typing class going?" Ida asked Darlene as they worked.

Darlene laughed ruefully. "I'll never break any speed records, Ida. But I'm learning the keyboard. That's what I wanted to do."

"I think you're pretty smart to even try."

"Smart?" Darlene scoffed. "I've *never* been described as smart." She pushed cotton down into the skinny tunnel that would magically become a doll's leg, and held it up. "Is this the way?"

Ida scrutinized Darlene's handiwork, then nodded. "A little more into the foot. You're getting the idea. Why do you think of yourself as dumb when you aren't, Darlene?"

She shrugged. "I don't know. I guess it's because I've done some really dumb things in my life."

"Well, heck, we've all done that." Ida shook her head and clucked her tongue. "I've done some really dumb things and made a few bad choices that I now regret. Bad decisions don't make you dumb, though. It just means your judgment was poor."

Darlene smiled at Ida. "You're great, you know that? I like being around you, Ida. You're good for the ego."

"You know something, Darlene? The feeling's mutual. Being around you makes me feel young again." Ida giggled self-consciously as if she were embarrassed by the admission. "I think you're going to be very good at this. You have a feel for doll making. It takes a special touch, and you've got it."

"It's really strange, Ida. Those little fellows seem to call to be made and finished." She nodded toward a lineup of doll forms spread out on the bed. "And when they're done, it's almost as if they're real . . . or sort of like cartoon characters that have come to life. It sounds crazy, I know."

"No, it doesn't." Ida grinned devilishly. "It means you're getting hooked."

"I'm hooked, all right. I've never done anything that was so compelling. Once I start to work on a doll, I hate to stop. And I can't wait to finish."

"My friend, Mary Beth, used to say that. She and I planned to go into the country doll-making business together before she moved to Knoxville," Ida said wistfully. "You talk about your mistakes, poor Mary

Beth made a big one in moving away. She isn't happy there at all."

"Then why doesn't she move back?"

"It isn't that easy to change your mind. She sold her home, so where would she go? She writes me long letters about how unhappy she is now." Ida sighed. "I wish I could help."

"Maybe Mary Beth needs some dolls to work on. Last night I worked until midnight on that one." Darlene gestured toward an unclothed, red-haired doll with long legs and big pearly-blue button eyes. "Just couldn't quit."

Curious, Ida picked the doll up and studied it. She was uncommonly silent. Darlene took the reaction to mean she didn't particularly care for the new-style doll.

"I realize that she's a little different from the ones we've been making. Longer arms and legs, which make her look bigger."

"And more real," Ida said softly.

"She has a certain personality, doesn't she? How do you think we should dress her?" Darlene looked up at the sound of footsteps on the porch. Her first thought—and hope—was that perhaps the visitor was Mac. "Someone's coming," she said, craning her head to see. "Oh, it's Boyd," she announced with surprise in her voice. He seldom came around.

Laying aside her work, Darlene headed for the door. She couldn't see the strange expression on Ida's face, but she did notice that Ida quickly hid the doll from view before Boyd could spot it.

"Hello, Boyd." Darlene stepped out onto the porch. "Ida's here. Are you looking for her?"

"Nope. Looking for you," he replied, casually leaning against the log railing that surrounded the porch. "I want you to know that I appreciate what you've done with cabin three...uh, the Crockett one. It looks great, plus the plumbing works. You're one clever lady, you know?"

"Well, thanks, Boyd." Darlene looked down at her feet, suddenly embarrassed by his compliments. "I guess that means I get to keep the job."

"Oh, yes, by all means. You've really perked things up around here, especially for Mama. She was busy with the kids, but lonely since her friend, Mary Beth, left."

"So I gathered."

"I hear you've also done a little work for Mac recently."

She looked up quickly. "I hope you don't mind, Boyd. He needed someone to take his scheduled tour. I made sure I was finished here. And Ida took calls for me."

"No, no. I don't mind. It gave me a chance to see that you have even more talents."

She frowned. "Fishing?"

"Yeah. Fishing and cooking."

"We just cooked what we caught."

"But you did it in style. Grilled trout and hush puppies. Why, it gave those folks something to talk—and brag—about for weeks to come. Sure would be nice if *we* could offer something like that."

"We? You mean—"

He nodded before she could finish. "Yep. Bear Creek Cabins could offer fishing tours, too. And we could beat the competition by having a fish fry at the end of the day."

"But the competition is Mac."

"Ah, not really. Several fellows around here offer fishing tours. Anyway, Mac's busy with his accounting jobs. Did you know he took over the books for that big trade-school in town?"

"Yes." Darlene licked her lips nervously. She didn't like the direction of the conversation. She couldn't imagine competing with Mac or doing anything that would hurt him.

"You don't seem too enthusiastic about the idea, Darlene."

"Well, I..."

Boyd held up one hand to stop her. "Think about this. I'll give you a raise in salary. You'd like that, wouldn't you?"

She nodded mutely.

"And I'll give you an additional commission for every tour you book." He gazed out into the woods, then back at her. "The way I look at it, there's plenty of fish for everybody. And there's plenty of people who want to fish. Now, why should Mac corner the market? No reason. It's a free country. Why should he keep you from doing what you want to do?"

"Well, I never considered adding fishing to my job here, Boyd."

"Think about it, Darlene. Don't make any rash decisions yet. Think about the money you could be making. It's an open market. Why not?" He ambled across the porch. "I'll be talking to you later about this."

Darlene stared at him with a sinking feeling in her stomach. How could she even consider such a thing? Why didn't she just tell Boyd outright—"No"? But she knew why. There was the unspoken threat to her job. Boyd was her boss, and she did what she was told—usually.

With a puzzled look on her face, Darlene reentered the room. Ida was staring at her. "He's my son, but sometimes I wonder where his head is. I can't imagine whatever possessed him to propose such a thing for you."

"You heard?"

"I hope you don't mind. I wasn't eavesdropping. The door was open."

Darlene shook her head. "I don't mind. I just can't imagine doing it, Ida."

"Well, you don't have to."

Darlene nodded silently. *Sure,* she thought. *Easy for you to say.* "He offered to increase my salary. Maybe then I could buy myself a car."

"You don't need a car. You can drive mine any time you want to."

"Thanks, but I can't keep driving your car, Ida. It just isn't right." She picked up the doll Ida had tucked beneath a corner of the quilt. "You don't like her, do you?"

Ida turned away. "Of course, I do."

"Then what's wrong?"

"Nothing. Just put a checkered dress on her, and she'll be fine."

"I don't want to put a checkered dress on her. I want her to be different."

"Dixie Johnson, who runs the Country Crafts Shop downtown, has agreed to buy dolls from us as long as they look like country folks."

"I don't want her to look ordinary. Help me make her look special, Ida."

"I can't."

"Why not?"

"Because she, uh, reminds me of someone. Remember how you felt when you first saw the doll that reminded you of Ken?"

"Yes." Darlene gazed solemnly at Ida. "Is she like a daughter?" she asked softly.

"Granddaughter."

"Oh. Where is she?"

Ida shrugged. "I think she's living in Nashville. Maggie left home several years ago, and we don't hear from her anymore."

"What happened? Did she run away?"

"Sort of." Ida laughed bitterly. "You talk about your bad decisions—that was a big mistake that I've always regretted."

"What, Ida?" Darlene sighed and looked away. "No, you don't have to tell me. This is obviously very private. And I have no right to press you about it."

Ida took a seat on the end of the bed near Darlene. "Maybe it'll make me feel better to tell someone who cares. You see, Maggie made a mistake. She got pregnant. And since she wasn't married, her family thought it was disgraceful. Boyd and his first wife, Maggie's mother, were awful. They disowned her, told her she'd disgraced them and she might as well leave because they weren't taking care of her brat. And I did nothing to stop it."

Darlene squeezed Ida's hand. "It wasn't your fault. What could you have done?"

"I could have provided a home for her. I should have stood up to Boyd and his wife. But I didn't. I will always regret that when Maggie needed someone, we weren't there for her. I'll never forgive myself." Ida wiped a tear from the corner of her eye.

"That's why you took over the care of Boyd's two younger children, isn't it?"

Ida nodded. "He's married a couple of strange women over the years. But now I feel that there's no reason for the kids to suffer. They had to have love and stability. Maybe I can provide for Emma and Byron what I didn't for Maggie."

"I think you're doing it." Darlene set the new doll on her knee and looked at her for a minute. "You know, I think Emma has the right idea. She has Sammi, her doll that's patterned after her mama. And I sort of like having Ken around me, even if he is in the form of a doll." She grinned at the perky, red-haired doll on her bed. "So, why don't we fix this one up for you? What would Maggie wear?"

Ida pressed her lips together and studied the doll. Finally she said, "Sequined jeans and a matching vest. Wild red hair and blue eyes. And a guitar. She wanted to be a professional singer and musician."

"Let me see what I can do with her. If you don't like her, we'll let Dixie Johnson sell her at the craft store. No problem."

Ida hesitated. Then she took the doll from Darlene and held it tightly to her breast. "Okay. Maybe it's a good idea to fix her up."

Darlene smiled warmly. She just knew that Ida would like the Maggie doll. Why, she already did. "You know something, Ida? I feel like I know Maggie. She and I have a lot in common. You see—" she paused "—I made a mistake, too. I had my son when I was still a child, myself. I was fifteen and unmarried."

"Did your family drive you away, too?" Ida looked at Darlene sympathetically, almost expecting her to relate a similarly sad tale.

"No. My mom took care of Ken until she died. And now, he lives with my brother, Chase. I have some regrets, too. I want to make it up to him. But I'm not sure how. Not yet. But I'll figure it out."

"I'm sure you will. But you're already showing him what he really wants, and that's love." Ida embraced Darlene, doll and all. "I knew there was some reason I liked you from the beginning." Their hug dissolved into giggly laughter and even a few tears, bonding them closer.

TWO DAYS LATER, Mac appeared at her door. When she saw his broad-shouldered outline in the late-afternoon light, she bounded to the door with joy and swung it open.

But the greeting she received was a scowl, not a smile. "Is this how you repay me? With competition for my business? Why don't you just take it over, Darlene? You can probably do it better than me, anyway. From what I've heard, you already did."

"What in the world are you talking about?"

He stalked into the room and looked around. He took a quick, deep breath and turned to face her. "Boyd says you're going to be offering fishing tours."

"I haven't decided yet—"

"Well, don't let me hold you back. In fact, how would you like a lesson in how to please even the clumsiest or most demanding customer? Or perhaps I could show you how to demonstrate fly-fishing, keeping the line doubled in the air for two full minutes. I'll show you all my tricks."

"Wait, wait." She held her hands up to stop him. "You're hitting me with this thing cold. Whatever Boyd told you isn't firm. Nothing has been decided."

"That's not what I heard."

"I was supposed to have time to think about it. I haven't made a decision. He just mentioned it to me the other day."

"Humph. Boyd thinks you've agreed to it. Anyway, he's offering you such a nice raise, you couldn't possibly refuse." Mac tossed a couple of brochures on the table. "Here's some info on taking the GED exam that I thought you might be interested in. But with your new business potential, you probably don't even want to bother with a test that gives you a high-school equivalency." He headed for the porch.

Mac was on the porch before Darlene could stop him. She stood in front of him with her hands on his wrists. "Hold on, Mr. Know-It-All! If you'll shut your mouth long enough to listen, you might learn my side of it! And yes, I'm very interested in the GED."

"Go ahead with your side." He clamped his jaw and tried not to look at her.

"Not here," she said quietly. "Inside."

He sighed heavily as if he were tolerating her.

"Come inside," she repeated in a low voice, "so I can see your face in the light. And we can talk. It's getting too dark out here."

His gaze softened ever so slightly. "Darlene, I don't care."

"Don't care?" Her heart pounded at the impact of his words. Did he mean that he didn't care about her?

"I honestly don't care if you can do better with these damned fishing tours than I have."

"That's a lie," she countered stoutly. "You just bit my head off for caring."

"I want . . . the best for you. If you want to, do it. Go for it."

"That's crazy. Who would say that to a competitor?"

"Someone who cared about his competitor."

She gazed at him in the growing darkness for a moment, then took him by the hand. "Let's go inside."

Mac heaved himself down into the cushioned chair. Darlene sat on the floor near his feet and leaned against the bed. "Okay, I'll tell you exactly what happened. Boyd did make me the offer. Lord knows why. All I did was take them fishing like you showed me to and cook it up afterward like you and I did that day after we saw the bear."

"That's it!" Mac exclaimed and gave his thigh a slap. "I don't have a fish fry. I never feed them."

"I didn't know. I thought you did. It just seemed the next logical thing to do."

"It's a good idea," he admitted with a grin. "You seem to be full of them."

She hugged her knees. "The only reason I hesitated to tell Boyd no was that I felt intimidated. He's my boss. And I had the impression that this was tied to my job. But I never intended to do anything to hurt you, Mac. Surely you know that by now."

Nervously he rubbed his thighs with his palms. "I realize that his offer must be tempting."

"The only reason I considered it was that I'd like to buy a car. And this would make it easier."

"I thought you wanted to make enough money to leave."

She lifted her face to him and her pain was clearly evident. "I...I thought so, too. But now, I don't know."

He reached out for her and immediately she pressed herself into his arms. "Oh, God, Darlene..." He kissed her hair, her forehead, her cheeks, her lips. "I don't want to even think about it," he murmured against her skin between kisses.

"Me either."

The moment of affection led to an hour of passion. Mac's kisses made her forget everything except his powerful physical presence. And his embrace gave her feelings of love and security that nourished her completely. Wedged between the strength of his thighs, she melted against him, thrilling to his desire.

Within minutes they were on the bed, kissing, holding, seeking. Sweet kisses led to touching. Touching led to caressing. Caressing became intimate stroking. And intimacy became a natural sharing of bodies, of passion, of love.

Mac stretched back on the bed while Darlene unbuttoned his shirt. With each button, she found a spot on his chest to kiss. She ran her fingers through the soft mat of curls, kissing his hot skin. She moved up to kiss his face and noticed the doll named Ken propped on the pillow. With its big eyes, it appeared to be watching them.

Responding to the unnerving realness of the doll, Darlene pushed it between the bed and the wall. *Out of sight, out of mind.*

Playfully Mac reversed their positions by rolling her onto her back and then began unbuttoning her sweater.

As he placed heated kisses on her exposed skin, she relaxed, knowing that they had complete and total privacy. No one was watching, especially not a doll that reminded her of her son. And when he slid the sweater off and pulled her jeans down, she could hardly wait for the fulfillment of their passion.

She fumbled with his belt, his zipper.

He helped. "Darlene. I don't know why I came over here angry."

"You have every right."

"I only wanted to hear one thing."

"I won't compete. You know that."

"That's not it."

"What, then?"

"That you'll stay—"

"I'll always be here for you. . . ."

"—for me *and* you." But his desire was overwhelming, too strong to deny or delay. With a low groan he filled her with his love.

She arched to meet his thrusts. Soft moans told him of her increasing pleasure. When they came, she had to admit that she loved him with her heart and soul, as well as her body. She shed sweet tears of happiness. She couldn't control them and didn't even try; just let them flow. And after the waves of their mutual ecstasy finally ebbed, she collapsed in his arms.

"Oh, Mac—" her voice was barely a whisper "—it doesn't get any better than this. . . ."

"Yeah. Not ever."

LATER THEY DECIDED to fix supper together. Darlene worked on the biscuits. Mac tackled the scrambled eggs.

"I guess it says something about our relationship if an argument could end in making love," she remarked with a laugh.

But Mac was serious. "I don't understand why I got so mad about this. You know I'd do anything for you, Darlene. I'd even give you my job."

"That's pretty generous of you." She mixed the dough, stirring it quickly with a fork. "But how would you support yourself?"

He shrugged. "I'd let you wear the pants, or the hip waders, as the case may be."

"Well, I can tell you right now, that won't be necessary. I have no intention of wearing the hip waders." She turned the dough out onto a floured board. "I'll tell Boyd my decision tomorrow."

"But your raise—"

"Who needs it? I can use Ida's car any time I want to."

"Or mine." Mac cracked half a dozen eggs into a bowl. "I used to be the kind of man who hated to lose. I was very competitive. Very honest and...ethical." He paused.

"I'm not surprised at that." She gave him a quick smile. "It's what I like so much about you."

"But no more."

"What do you mean? You're the most honest man I know."

"Honest, yes. But I don't function with those old standards anymore."

"Why?"

"They don't work."

"Of course, they do. Decency and honesty are the foundation of the work ethic in this country."

"They didn't work for me. That's why I'm here."

"They're why you lost your job at the coal mine?" she asked softly, knowing she was treading on sensitive ground.

"Yep."

"What happened? I assumed there were layoffs, and you were one of them. That's the usual scenario in the mining business."

"Not this time. I did it to myself."

A strange expression spread over his face. This was a part of Mac that Darlene had never seen. She was suddenly disturbed by what he was saying. She shoved the panful of biscuits into the oven, then sat at the table, turning her full attention to him.

He sat down across from her and folded his arms in front of him. "I guess it's time you knew about my sordid past. It might change your opinion of things. Maybe even of me."

"I doubt it." She gave him a confident smile, knowing that she had a hidden past that would probably surpass anything he could tell her. Someday she would tell him. She had to. But not now. His thick brown hair glistened in the kitchen light and his blue eyes darkened as he began to talk. Darlene thought he was the most handsome man she'd ever seen—or loved—and nothing he could say would change that.

"I was the production accountant at the mine," he began. "Which means I measured the amount of bulk coal that came out of the tunnel. Everything we produced was accounted for by me. Those production figures became the basis for the profit-and-loss statement for the entire mine. One time I saw a draft of the quarterly report and questioned its accuracy with my boss. Basically he told me to keep quiet about it. I was shocked."

"Why didn't he want to fix the mistakes?"

Mac shrugged. "Obviously he was hiding something. When the final report was released, the figures were still inaccurate. So I skirted my immediate boss and went to the mine manager with my information. He said that I should do my job and leave the quarterly reports alone."

"He must have been hiding something, too."

"Exactly. They were hiding profits. I'm not sure how far up the corporate ladder it went, because I was fired the next day."

"For what? Didn't you tell them what you saw?"

"Oh, yes. But every word I said after that just made things worse." He shook his shaggy head. "They could have benefited from figuring production low by paying less tax. Then, the excess could have been awarded in bonuses. Or they could have been skimming directly off the unlisted profits, along with other top executives of the company. I don't know. Because I was out."

"Mac, I'm sorry."

"Don't be. I'm better off now. But I was in desperate shape for a long time. My marriage was falling apart. And nobody would hire a whistle-blower. I was poison." He sighed heavily. "Then I decided to make some major changes. I let the mining industry go, let the marriage go, piled everything into my car and left town."

She smiled gently. "I've done that a few times, too. But somehow I never landed on my feet like you have, Mac."

"You're doing great."

"Not until this time. You've helped."

"Helped? Why, when you arrived in town, I'd never seen such a stubborn, self-reliant person in my life. You didn't need anybody's help, much less mine. And you were quick to tell me."

"I was bluffing."

"That's the first step to making it, didn't you know? You've got to convince yourself you're going to make it." He grinned, and she came around the table and slid into his arms.

"I'm proud of you, Mac Jackson. I don't care if you did lose your job. What you did was honest and...noble."

"And pretty stupid. It cost me dearly to point out others' mistakes. But you know, I don't regret it. Not for a minute. Because if I hadn't ended up here, I wouldn't have met you, darlin'."

She bent down and kissed him deeply. After a long, sensual moment, she gasped and pushed away.

"The biscuits are burning!" She scrambled toward the stove.

He threw open the back door to allow the smoke to escape.

Fifteen minutes later they were eating scrambled eggs and toast. Most of the smoke was gone. The biscuits had been tossed out.

"You know something, Mac?" Darlene took a bite of egg and chewed slowly. "I feel as if I'm starting over, too, just like you did. I don't have the same problems as you, but they're equally paralyzing to me. When I arrived here, I had nowhere else to turn."

He nodded understandingly. "When I arrived here, the people accepted me as I was. There were no pretenses between us. They'll accept you, too, Darlene. Once you get to know more folks and stick around here awhile, you'll see why I like it so much. Why I intend to stay." He glanced across the table at her. "I hope you will, too."

She gulped and took a swallow of hot chocolate. "I plan to study for my GED. I think they give the test in the fall."

"Will you still be here then?"

She looked at him steadily and smiled ever so slightly. "Yes, of course."

"Good." He turned his attention to his food.

It was midnight before Mac left.

Sitting alone in the room, Darlene felt empty and deceiving. Now would be a good time for a smoke. Lord, the craving was suddenly so strong she could taste it! Thank goodness there were no cigarettes on the premises, or she would lose the bet tonight.

She felt as if she were living a lie with Mac. He'd been totally honest with her, revealing a hidden secret that he hated. But she hadn't done the same. Her secret was still festering. And it threatened to destroy them.

She loved him—and was afraid, because she didn't know what to do about it; afraid because she was committed to returning to Arkansas and to her son.

The emotion pulling her back was stronger than ever. Stronger than anything she'd ever known. A mother needed to be near her son. And a son needed to know his mom, even if she hadn't been the greatest.

Darlene flopped on the bed. She felt like crying. She remembered where she'd stuffed the doll and reached behind the bed for it. Hugging it tightly to her breast, she wept. "Oh, Ken, I love you," she murmured. "And I want to prove it. But how? Things are getting so complicated. Too complicated."

8

DARLENE WAITED NERVOUSLY for Ida. The Maggie doll, all decked out in a glittering denim outfit, lay on the bed as if waiting for Ida, too.

Darlene was pleased with the way the doll had turned out. But she was as nervous as a long-tailed cat in a roomful of rocking chairs about Ida's reaction. What would she think of the doll? What if she didn't like it at all? What if the memories it generated of her absent granddaughter were too painful?

Making the Maggie doll had been an act of love for Darlene. She wanted it to cheer Ida and hoped her friend would like it. She stared lovingly at the doll she'd named after Ken. For herself, having that doll had somehow made her son seem a little closer. It certainly made her think of him often and reminded her to write him more frequently.

She shared many things in her life with Ken now, which she'd never done before. Now, though, she was doing things she was proud of, like learning to type. She told him about Ida and the two kids, Emma and Byron, and even about her "friend," Mac. Ken wrote frequently, too, keeping her posted on his activities in Arkansas. Mother and son were closer now than they'd ever been, and Darlene was very happy about that.

She couldn't help feeling that the doll had something to do with this improvement in her relationship with Ken. She wasn't sure why, but she had special feelings for all the dolls she made. Since she'd started making them, she experienced a strange and distinct phenomenon as each one reached completion. It was almost as if each doll suddenly came alive with a personality of its own.

She felt as if she were creating a perfect little world—one where there were no problems, no sadness, no separated families. In fact, the dolls themselves were almost like a family. The thought of selling them sometimes made Darlene shudder. And yet, that was the purpose of making them. She had agreed to help Ida supply the crafts shop with dolls to sell. And they'd already sold a few.

She glanced at the Maggie doll with its sequined jeans and vest and wildly curly hair, and she smiled. She couldn't help it. The doll just made her cheerful. Maybe Darlene could clone this one and make other versions of the Maggie doll to sell. She also liked her own cute Ken. She felt sure these dolls would give others the same pleasures they gave her. She could even make a family—a whole family for her perfect world. A mom and dad and kids....

Suddenly, Darlene grabbed her notebook and a pencil and started scribbling furiously. By the time Ida arrived, she had several pages of notes and drawings.

She greeted Ida with a breathless glow. "Hi! Come on in and see what I've been doing!"

Ida responded to Darlene's enthusiasm with a smile. "What have you been up to, girl?"

Darlene giggled nervously. "I'll show you. But first, I have the doll for you . . . the Maggie doll. Oh, Ida, I hope you like it. If not, though, I do, so I'll keep her. Or we'll just send her to the shop for sale. But I hope—"

Ida propped her hands on her hips. "Would you quit jabbering and show her to me?"

Somberly Darlene handed Ida the doll.

Ida held it at arm's length for a moment, then turned it over, examining it quietly. Finally, she looked up. There was a strained expression on her face and huge tears filled her eyes. Then she smiled. "She's beautiful. Just like my Maggie."

"But . . . do you like her?"

"Of course, I do!"

Darlene burst into relieved laughter. "I'm so glad to hear that!"

Ida hugged Darlene warmly. "Why wouldn't I like her? She reminds me of my two favorite people. You and Maggie. Besides, I like everything you do, Darlene."

"Oh, now, Ida . . ." Darlene brushed off her compliment with a blush of embarrassment.

Ida stood back and eyed the doll, then Darlene. "You have quite a talent, here, girl. You have a way of making these dolls come alive like I've never seen. Mary Beth couldn't do it. I certainly couldn't."

"Ida, I don't know what you're talking about. Why, you're the one who showed me how to make them."

"Not like this, I didn't. Look at that face. It's amazing how only big button eyes can look so endearing. And those long legs and arms take the dolls out of the baby-doll stage, yet they're still cuddly. The clothes, though, really do make the doll an individual. You've taken the basics and made your own individual creations. And that's a very special talent. Don't let it go to waste."

"I'm not. I want to save this Maggie."

"What's wrong with her?" Ida gazed at the long-legged doll in her hands. "She looks okay to me."

"Oh, she is," Darlene went on enthusiastically. "She's great. She's such a terrific character, I'd like to clone her."

"Clone Maggie?" Ida looked puzzled. "You mean, make more of her?"

"Uh-hmm, if you don't mind. We could name the new one something else, like Sugar. Sugar Britches. And she'd be a part of the Britches family." Darlene took Ida's arm and pulled her toward the table and the notes she'd made. "I just want to use this prototype because she's so cute. We'll change her. In fact, I want every doll to be different, even if only in her clothes. That's what will make each one an individual."

"You mean, each one would be an original?"

Darlene shrugged. "Whatever."

"Well, you don't have to have my approval," Ida said.

"Oh, yes, I do. Because I want to make a . . ." Darlene paused and picked up the notebook. "I want to make a whole family of dolls. The Britches family. With a ma and pa and a girl sort of like Maggie and a boy kind of like Ken. Here. Take a look."

Ida studied the notes and drawings Darlene had made. With encouragement, she began to make suggestions about possible alterations. Her enthusiasm grew as she added her own ideas to Darlene's originals. Darlene noticed with pride that Ida unconsciously tucked the Maggie doll onto her lap and hugged it as they pored over the notebook.

For the next two hours each contributed ideas for the new creations. They decided that Ma Britches would have a calico dress and apron; Pa Britches would wear overalls and "smoke" a corncob pipe; Billy Bob Britches would be barefoot, with a fishing pole over his shoulder and Sugar Britches would wear flashy jeans and a Paisley vest. She would be the contemporary member of the Britches family.

Suddenly they realized that they had forgotten all about lunch. Ida got up. "Omigosh, it's time for Emma and Byron to come home from school! Where did this day go? I've got to get home. See you tomorrow."

Darlene walked her to the door. "Okay. We'll work on the family then."

Ida paused. "Thanks for my Maggie, Darlene. I'll always treasure her." Smiling, Ida clutched the Maggie doll to her breast and hurried through the woods to her house. It was the most excited Darlene had ever seen Ida. And the happiest.

This was the most creative she had ever been, and it was liberating. With Ida's encouragement, she was discovering an aspect of herself that she never knew existed—and that she liked very much.

MAC PICKED A SPOT in the far corner of Darlene's backyard and spread the blanket. They weren't far from Bear Creek.

Darlene carefully placed the chocolate cake in the center of the blanket. "There. I dare that bear to come after our cake this time."

Mac handed her the bag of sandwiches and chips. "I doubt if he'll come to this side of the creek. It's too close to the cabins and civilization. But just in case, we'll make our share of noise to keep him scared away." Mac set a portable radio on the blanket and tuned in a music station.

"I'll skin me a b'ar if he comes around here!" Darlene knotted her fist and shook it in the air. "You hear that, bear?"

Laughing at her performance, Mac grabbed her and pulled her lovingly into his arms. "Boy, you sure sound tough. But when it comes to rough action, you're a pussycat."

She pretended to fight with him until his kiss left her breathless and weak. Clinging to his shoulders, she smiled up at him. "You're not so tough, either."

"Not when it comes to you."

"I know your ulterior motive. You just want some of my Scrumptious Chocolate Fudge Cake."

"Hmm, and that's not all." He kissed her again, long and hard.

Finally she muttered something about eating lunch before the squirrels found their Scrumptious Chocolate Fudge Cake, and reluctantly he agreed.

Mac handed her a turkey sandwich. "One of the specialties of the Jackson house."

"You cook?"

"Well, a guy's gotta do something when he's on his own. This isn't an ordinary roasted turkey. It's smoked to perfection." He kissed his fingertips. "Also, the sandwich spread is my own gourmet concoction."

She looked surprised. "You smoked your own turkey?"

"It's no big deal. The smoker, which is sort of like a barbecue grill, does the work."

"Then you could smoke the fish you catch."

He nodded. "Of course. Never tried it, but it could be done."

She grinned. "When you start offering a fish dinner after the tour."

"Only if you'll do the hush puppies."

"Sure. I'll consider it for a consultant's fee." She rolled her eyes. "Boyd'll really like that."

He motioned to her sandwich. "Would you please taste my fabulous homemade sauce?"

Darlene took a bite of the sandwich that Mac had prepared. The heat from the sauce hit her tongue, went immediately to her throat, then sent vapors steaming through her nose. She muffled a cough and chewed rapidly, then blew her breath out, panting as she gasped, "Whoa! It's really hot!"

Mac smiled proudly. "Yeah. Great, isn't it? My secret is fresh horseradish."

Feverishly she popped the top of a canned drink and gulped several times. "Horseradish. I'll remember that. Yes, indeedy."

"But I'm not revealing *all* the ingredients. A man's gotta have some secrets."

"Aww. I was hoping to drag it out of you." She grabbed the bag of chips and tore into them. "But I guess everybody's gotta have some secrets."

"For you, I might make an exception."

"No, no! I wouldn't dare force the secret from you."

"Are you saying that you don't want it?"

"Well, it *is* pretty hot." She braced herself for another bite. "But good. Very tasty."

As they bantered playfully, Darlene thought of her own dark secret, one that might tear them apart. And yet, the longer she kept it from him, the worse she felt. She had to tell him. Soon.

Mac launched into another subject, and she readily went along. "And this teacher at the Trade and Craft School conducts a class tutoring kids, er, people, who want to take the GED exam."

"Well, it *is* mostly people younger than me who want to take the exam and complete their education."

"True. But the point is that the class is open to everyone." Mac paused. "He says it starts in September. Will you still be here then?"

It was a simple enough question, but Darlene stumbled around, trying to answer it. "I...uh, I'm sure...I, uh, guess so. I don't have enough money saved to consider moving yet." She crunched a chip. "I'd like to take that course. I know I'm going to need tutoring, especially in math."

Without pursuing the subject further, they finished their sandwiches in silence. Mac eagerly went for the cake, slicing two huge chunks. "Now I get to see why our uninvited furry friend liked it so much. Thanks for making it again." He took a bite, then began to rave about it. "The name is accurate. It's certainly scrumptious! But what is this white stuff in the middle of the chocolate? A secret ingredient?"

"The filling? It's cream cheese, coconut and chocolate chips," Darlene answered.

"What? You're telling me your secret ingredients so easily? Now I feel guilty for keeping mine."

She shrugged. "I guess I feel there are enough secrets between us."

"Like what? I've revealed all my wicked past." He leaned back on one elbow and picked at the cake. "So, tell me yours."

Darlene swallowed hard and gazed at him. He was having such a good time and was in such high spirits, she just couldn't face the prospect of destroying the wonderful mood they shared. Instead, she launched into her doll making. "I have another project to keep me busy and, hopefully, improve my income considerably."

"What's that?"

"Doll making. Ida and I are going to make dolls for sale at Dixie's craft shop."

"I think you mentioned that."

"But Ida and I have a new plan. This is completely different. We're designing a family of country dolls." Her enthusiasm grew as she talked about their plans. "Making dolls does strange things to the creator. It's like inventing a miniature world, a perfect one that's so different from the real world. This one is always happy and fun and available."

Mac listened closely as Darlene explained details of the Britches family. He could almost feel her excitement as she talked of the demand for country dolls in the Gatlinburg area. When she launched into methods of making the dolls unique in the marketplace, he knew she'd done her homework.

"Sounds like you and Ida have a good saleable idea."

"We think so." Darlene hugged her knees. "But you know, it's funny. I think I'd do this even if the market wasn't so receptive. I love the ability to create my own little family. You probably aren't going to believe this, but the dolls actually have a personality by the time I'm finished with them."

"Darlene, can you pull this off? Can you and Ida actually supply enough dolls to sell and make it profitable?"

"I believe it's possible. They're not very complicated to make, although they are time-consuming. Ida can make the doll form in a few hours, and I can dress one—if I have all the materials—in an hour or less. Let me show you what I've done."

Before Mac could respond, Darlene was dashing back to her cabin for the Sugar Britches doll. Mac watched her sprint across the wooded backyard. He'd never seen her so eager. Nor had he seen her so happy since she'd arrived that night with a big bruise on her face and a scared desperateness about her. He didn't know much about the market for dolls, but obviously she and Ida had studied it. Most important, Darlene had found something that made her happy.

Inside the cabin, Darlene grabbed her newest creation, Sugar Britches, just finished this morning. Ida hadn't even seen this one, who wore tight jeans and a bright Paisley vest. She spotted her beloved Ken doll on the bed and, for no clear reason, grabbed him up, too.

When Darlene returned, she lovingly told Mac about the Maggie doll she'd made for Ida and who the real Maggie was. She related how that one doll had generated ideas to expand the concept to a whole family of dolls.

Then Darlene picked up the Ken doll and stared at the sweet, animated face. It was almost as if the doll had made his presence known, had forced her to bring him along. There was more to tell Mac. She couldn't avoid it any longer. *Now was the time.* "It all started with this one," she said, handing it to Mac.

He held it in one large hand, then looked curiously at Darlene. "What started?"

"The doll making. Ida left this half-finished form in the closet. She showed me how to finish the doll. Only I made it into a boy, instead of a girl as she'd expected." Darlene paused and fiddled with the doll's shoe. "I'm not exactly sure why I made it this way, but I have a pretty good idea. A psychologist would probably jump on that one pretty quickly with some answers. Anyway, I liked this doll and named him . . . Ken, after someone who's very dear to me. And that's why I figured that Ida would like her Maggie doll."

"What are you trying to say, Darlene? That Ken is someone real?"

She nodded, licking her lips nervously, and then hurried on before she lost her nerve. "I know I've waited too long to tell you this, Mac. But it has to come out. I didn't tell you because I was afraid I'd lose you. But secrets aren't the way to build a relationship—truth is. And the truth is . . . Ken is my son. The reason I want to go back to Arkansas is because my son is there.

Mac stared, speechless. Angry thoughts raged through him. Why hadn't she told him before now? Now, when he really cared for her. Now, when he considered her the best thing that had ever happened to him. Now, when he entertained the possibility of loving her.

Mac was stunned.

Darlene felt the need to fill the uncomfortable silence. "So, how can I promise you that I won't leave, Mac? I have a son in Arkansas. I want to be near him, and I'd like to think he wants me near him, too."

"How could you keep something like that from me?" Mac tossed the doll onto the blanket and glared at her. "How could you lead me on like this? Of all the dirty tricks—" He was on his feet.

Darlene stood to face him. "It's not a dirty trick. I wanted to tell you. But every time I got up my nerve, something stopped me."

"Something *conveniently* came up?"

"No. But I . . ."

He turned away from her and started toward the stream and home.

She went after him. "Wait, Mac. Listen to me!"

He slowed, and she caught up with him beside the stream. "Listen to my side of this, dammit!"

He halted and stood stiffly, looking straight ahead.

She caught his wrists as if she could hold him back. She knew that was impossible. "Please let me tell you about Ken and me." The closed expression on his face told her he wasn't receptive.

Still, she plunged ahead. "I had Ken when I was fifteen. I was just a kid and not ready for such a huge responsibility. My mother took care of the baby and me, and when I decided to leave home, she begged me to leave Ken with her. She loved him. And I knew that she could take better care of him than I could. So I let him stay in Arkansas." She wiped away her tears and continued with her story. "After Mama died, my brother, Chase, took care of Ken. I... Now, I'd like to make it up to Ken somehow. And," she added softly, "I'd like to make him proud of me."

Mac ran his hand through his hair and looked away from her. "That's a sweet story, Darlene. But it's all too familiar to me. I've been this route before, and while it's great for you, it doesn't work for me."

"It's not a *sweet story.*" She stamped her foot impatiently. "It's not perfect. But it's real life. It's my life, and I won't apologize. I thought maybe with your help and understanding, I—"

"Uh-uh! Count me out. You know how I feel about this, Darlene."

She folded her arms and tightened her jaw. "I was hoping you'd join us. But I won't leave my son out of my life. Now you know how I feel about it."

"I can tell you from experience, there's no place for a third wheel on a two-wheel cart." He turned and hopped from rock to rock as he crossed the stream.

"We aren't talking about carts. We're talking about people!" Darlene shouted to him from the edge of the stream. "You're a damn fool, Mac Jackson! A damn, stubborn fool!"

He didn't respond, but kept going.

Darlene returned to the picnic site and began picking up the pieces. The sandwich wrappers. The chips.

The remaining Scrumptious Chocolate Fudge Cake. The dolls. *The secrets.*

It took her four trips to lug it all inside. She piled what was left of the picnic on the table and carefully placed the two dolls on the end of her bed. She didn't cry at all until she looked at the Ken doll. Of all the dumb luck! She had fallen in love with a man who could never love her son.

"DARLENE? YOU HOME?" Ida called out.

Darlene heard Ida's voice. She swiped the tears from her cheeks. "Yes?"

Ida appeared in the dark doorway. "I hope I'm not interrupting anything. I can come back another time."

"No, no. It's all right. Come on in."

Ida stepped into the semidark room. Darlene was curled up on the bed, hiding her feelings in the growing darkness. Reluctantly she switched on the light.

"Is something wrong?"

"Nothing that you can fix, Ida." She motioned with one hand as if to hurry Ida. "What is it?"

Ida stepped closer to the bed. "I'd hoped you'd be excited about my news. But I suppose nothing could be exciting to you right now."

"What news?" she asked impatiently.

"Every fall, we have the Blue Ridge Artists and Crafters Fair. It's coming in mid-October. There'll be all kinds of contests, including a special prize this year for the best native mountain craft."

"So?"

"Well, it would seem the almost-perfect place for you to enter the country Britches family." Ida paused as she tried to ignore Darlene's red eyes and blotchy face. "First prize is a thousand dollars. That'd be more than enough to fly you home to Arkansas."

Darlene nodded sullenly. "You may be right, Ida. I might as well go for it. There's no more need to stay around here."

"Oh, honey, it's Mac, isn't it?" Ida came over and sat on the edge of the bed. She slid her arm around Darlene's shoulders. "I know it's none of my business, but sometimes a woman knows. And understands best."

"It's Mac, all right!" Darlene exploded angrily. "He's so damn... pigheaded and... stubborn! And uncaring."

"Well, I won't argue with you," Ida said wryly. "Except on that last one. I think he cares even more than he knows."

"No, you're wrong. He's made of stone. I won't— No, I *can't* back down on this, Ida. But he refuses to even listen, to even try to understand my side of it. He doesn't care about my feelings." Darlene paused for a long minute and gathered her nerve. "I told him about Ken. My son."

"I guess that was a pretty big shock."

"Shock? He was electrified!"

Ida clucked her tongue against her teeth and shook her head. "Too bad he's so dead set. Why, he doesn't even know your son."

"He's really a neat kid."

Ida patted her hand. "Give Mac time to adjust, girl. Give him time."

"He's got until fall."

"Then what?"

"Oh, I don't know, Ida," she moaned. "I just don't know."

"A word of advice, girl. Don't give up your son. Not for anybody. You'll regret it the rest of your life."

"I know. And I don't intend to give him up. Not now."

Long after Ida left, Darlene mulled over their conversation. Ida understood and accepted her feelings as a mother. Mac simply refused to.

No apologies, no regrets. That was the philosophy on which their relationship had been built. Until now, it had worked. Now, though, Mac was refusing to enter a very important part of her life. She wanted him by her side, supportive. She wanted Ken to know Mac, to like him.

But Darlene knew that Ida was right. She couldn't bear to have any more regrets about her own son. There had been already too many over the past twelve years. She was through apologizing for her mistakes and her life. She was ready to face her past, to own up and make things better.

But was she prepared to give up Mac in order to accomplish this, her biggest goal?

Tears overflowed her eyes as she knew the inevitable answer.

But something Ida had said haunted her: *Why, he doesn't even know your son.* Darlene sat upright on the bed as an idea struck her. And there was only one way for it to happen. She'd talk to Chase. Maybe he would be willing to help.

9

DARLENE KNEW HER PLAN was devious...even wicked. But that's what made it exhilarating.

She couldn't make things worse. Her relationship with Mac was down the tubes. There was no turning back. A swift breeze lifted her hair and tossed it carelessly around her head. She walked a little faster in an effort to beat the approaching rain.

Her plan was to seduce Mac with every ounce of charm she could muster. Then she'd make him listen to her, make him understand her viewpoint. *Make him?* She shuddered involuntarily. Could she actually *make* Mac Jackson do anything?

Darlene squared her shoulders and increased her speed. That was the challenge. She wasn't the manipulative type. She was too straightforward for it. Too straightforward for her own good.

The first drops of rain peppered the dry leaves like rice falling on parchment paper. Darlene moved faster along the road. Oh, sure, she was still angry at Mac. He'd been so thoughtless and narrow-minded about the whole thing. And yes, she was a little scared. Scared of losing him. She just had to win him over. Had to try.

She felt a few drops hit her head and she started to jog. The heavy fragrance of new moisture mingled with layers of dust on the dry leaves and earth. She stopped long enough to remove her shoes. Even though this would ruin her new hose, she couldn't run in high heels.

As Darlene raced along, getting wetter by the minute, it occurred to her that the rain changed things. No longer would she look attractive and sultry. The hour spent creating the curly side-sweep hairdo was wasted as the whole mess began to fall apart, pin by pin. Soon she was soaked and her hair flopped like a soggy scarf on her neck.

Maybe—she was panting now—maybe it would be better this way. Her brain shifted into gear with a new plan....

By the time Darlene knocked on Mac's door and heard Ace's welcoming bark, her scoop-neck blouse was plastered to her body. Her hair dripped on her shoulders. And she could feel mud squishing around her toes through her torn stockings. She was going to seduce someone like this?

Mac opened the door and stared at Darlene. Water streamed down her face, and mascara dribbled like black tears beneath each soulful eye. Her thin, wet blouse molded to every sensuous curve. Her hair hung in limp ribbons. She was an awful mess, but beautiful and—oh, Lord—sexy!

She was panting and shivering at the same time, and Mac's blood quickened as he stood looking at her. Then he remembered their argument. He couldn't let himself have tender feelings for her. He couldn't forget her deception.

Tonight, though, there was a certain expression in her large, chestnut eyes that moved him. It was a look he'd seen before—desperation mixed with fear. As always, however, her true feelings were masked by a definite brashness of demeanor. Darlene's trademark.

"Darlene, what the—"

She propped one fist, clutching a high-heeled shoe, on her hip. "I came over to talk."

He almost laughed. "Tonight? Poor timing, huh?"

"What we have at stake doesn't merit your feeble jokes, Mac," she said with a toss of her head. Droplets sprinkled him and Ace, who howled and backed up.

"Who's joking?" Mac mumbled and stepped back, too.

Darlene glared at him, her eyes determined and unblinking. "You wouldn't have company tonight, would you, Mac?"

There was no answer. Just a dark, disgusted look on his face. He gestured with a quick nod for her to enter. His mouth was set, and his bearded jaw quivered from a muscle spasm as he watched her move toward him and begin to methodically strip off her clothes.

"I'll, uh, get a towel," he offered hurriedly. By the time he returned, a large fluffy towel in hand, she stood stark naked in his open doorway. Mac stared. She was gorgeous!

Grimly smiling, Darlene took the towel from him and dabbed it over her body, then squeezed the tips of her hair with it. With a little fling, she threw it over one shoulder, not bothering with modesty. "Thanks," she murmured and glided across the room. Her bare feet left dark prints on the rug.

Mac watched her hips sway for a weak-willed moment, then scooped up her wet clothes and headed for the kitchen. "I'll dry these. Would you like some dry clothes?"

"Nope. Not this time." Darlene positioned herself on the sofa, the towel casually—and sexily—covering her body. She stretched her long, tanned legs across the cushions with a brazen, feminine confidence. "I'm kind of surprised to find you here, Mac. After all, it *is* Friday night."

He sat on the edge of the seat in the chair opposite her. Leaning forward, he propped his elbows on his knees and gestured with his hands between them. Her leg was close enough to touch, and it was all he could do to keep from reaching out. "You know me, Darlene. I don't go for that kind of life-style. Anyway, I, uh, had two fishing tours today and needed to repair some of my gear tonight."

"Did you get everything all fixed?"

He nodded, then eyed her suspiciously. Why was she making small talk? It made him nervous. "You aren't usually off on weekends, Darlene. You didn't quit your job, did you?" Suddenly his mouth tasted like metal. What if she'd quit and was heading back to Arkansas?

She merely smiled. "I asked Ida to take my calls. I figured I'd be gone all night. Do you work tomorrow?"

"I have two tours again."

"Too bad. Hope you aren't too tired."

He chuckled sourly. "Darlene, what are you up to?"

"Like I said, I'm here to talk." She gazed around the room. "You know, a fire would be nice. And some brandy."

"Brandy?" He looked surprised. This wasn't like her at all. "I don't happen to have brandy in my liquor cabinet," he drawled. "Would a light Chardonnay do?"

"Of course. Anything." Darlene felt the need for fortification about now.

Mac moved slowly toward the fireplace, knowing she had this whole thing planned—and that he was the fly in her spiderweb. Furthermore, he was a willing victim. He couldn't help himself.

Ten minutes later, Darlene stood and tucked the towel around her. It barely covered her torso, which was perfect for her plan. With the fire blazing behind her, she raised her wineglass in a toast. "To a humdinger of a summer love affair, Mac Jackson," she said caustically. "You're one helluva lover. The best I've known. It's been fun."

He touched her wineglass with his and muttered, "Sarcasm doesn't become you, Darlene."

"Why should you care what does or doesn't become me?" She leaned her head back and tossed down a sizable amount of wine. The more she spoke, the bolder she became. It was the only way she could handle this.

"Because... I care. That's all."

"Funny statement coming from someone who can't stand the truth."

"Darlene—"

"I'm trying to understand you, Mac. Why is the truth so tough for you to handle?" She took another large swallow and set the half-finished glass on a table. The movement loosened the towel, and she clutched it to her as she walked past him. Her rear was completely bare.

"I figure it's because you want things your way—and only your way. Or it's over, huh?"

"No one said that, Darlene." He set his wineglass down and watched her. So she wanted to play games? "Don't overlook the fact that you are the one who deceived me. It was like lying."

She whirled to face him. "I never lied to you. I only gave you what I knew you wanted to hear."

"Ha! What an unusual view of things—strictly from your side, of course."

"My biggest mistake wasn't in getting pregnant at fifteen, or leaving my kid with my family to raise or even in not telling you. Those things happened, and I did the best I could under the circumstances. No, Mac. My biggest mistake was in loving you. I trusted you. I thought you'd understand—"

He moved swiftly to her, grabbing her forearms. "Stop it! This isn't love. It's some sort of . . . revenge. What kind of game are you playing here?"

She squirmed out of his grasp, somehow managing to hang on to the towel. "What did you expect I'd do when you rejected my kid?" Tossing her damp hair, she flicked droplets that sizzled when they hit the fire. "I'm a mother. And I won't turn my back on my son anymore. Not for you, not for . . . anyone." Darlene could feel the hard knot of emotion growing in her chest. She wanted to burst, to scream. But she couldn't let down. Not yet.

"I . . . I need some time to think about this, Darlene. To adjust to the idea. You hit me cold. You have to admit that."

"How long?"

"Huh?" He watched her adjust the towel so that it hung over one shoulder, exposing most of her in an extremely provocative way.

"How long do you need to think about it? A couple of days or a couple of years?"

"Uh, I, uh, don't know."

"Well, I'd like to know something tonight." She walked across the room to the table where he'd been working. When she moved, the towel flopped gently on one silky hip and the smooth curve of her back. Gingerly she touched different pieces of his fishing gear on the table.

"You're asking too much."

"I'd like to know where I stand with you, Mac." She whirled around with a smile, letting the towel flap carelessly about her body. She continued her seductive dance about the room, moving slowly at times, touching various objects—the desk, the typewriter, a fishing rod propped in the corner. "Is that too much to ask tonight?" She grabbed his tattered green fishing hat, the one studded with a dozen or so dry flies, and stuck it on her head. "I've already admitted my love for you, wasted though it may be."

He swallowed hard. She looked so incongruous—and so damned sexy—in that hat with feathered dry flies and wearing only a towel. "It...uh, it isn't wasted. You know I care for you, Darlene. And I—" His voice stuck like gravel in his throat for a minute. "I'm sorry I hurt you."

"How sweet," she murmured sarcastically. "I admit my love and you admit you care. Let's get real, Mac."

He continually turned to keep her in sight as she moved about the room. He'd never seen her like this. She was seductive and vicious at the same time. He couldn't keep his eyes off the skin she was exposing as she wove between his furniture. Finally, in frustration, he gasped, "If you'd be still, dammit, maybe we could talk!" He was grasping for some sort of control . . . but losing it. Actually, this evening he'd never really had it. From the moment she'd stepped in the door, she was in charge.

"Sure, Mac. Anything you say." Darlene reversed a wooden, straight-back chair, straddled it and propped her forearms on its back. "Go ahead. Talk. I know you're angry with me. You must have lots of things bottled up." She adjusted the fishing hat to a jaunty angle.

Mac was amazed that she hadn't lost her towel as she climbed onto that chair. The damn thing draped from one shoulder down the length of her torso to the tops of her thighs. Both bare legs jutted out from either side of the towel, which covered her just enough to leave everything else to his imagination. He sat down again and swallowed, trying to remember what it was that he had wanted to say to her. Right now, his brain was definitely muddled. His one concern was how to confiscate that towel!

"Well?" She tapped one bare foot impatiently. "Go ahead."

"I, uh . . ." He paused, then tried to continue: "You know, Darlene, that I've had a really bad experience with, uh, someone else's kid. I swear he was the root cause of the breakup of our marriage. And I . . . we wanted that marriage to work. But the problems he created were . . . He pitted us against each other . . . and me against him . . . and therefore against his mother . . . my wife . . . uh, former wife."

"One kid did all that?"

"Well—"

Darlene nodded solemnly. "That was indeed a bad scene. So now you hate all kids, right?"

"Well, no . . ."

"Just some?"

"No!"

"So, what does that have to do with us?"

"I don't want the same thing to happen again. To us, Darlene."

"So you want no kids in the picture."

"I just see me relating to a strange kid and a strange kid adjusting to me as being—"

"Insurmountable?" she filled in when he paused. "Gee, that's funny. You always encouraged me to do things beyond my ability and to see them through. You said nothing was impossible if you wanted to make it happen."

"Well, it's different when you're talking about taking a class or doing something to improve your situation." He reached for his abandoned wineglass. At the moment, he wished he'd poured something stronger, like a stiff shot of Jack Daniel's whiskey. "This is real life I'm talking about. Relationships. Real adult problems."

"I've had just about as much experience with 'real life' as you have, Mac. Maybe more." She shoved the fishing hat back on her head with her thumb. "And I believe that nothing is beyond a little hard work. And a little tough love."

He finished his wine in one large gulp and set the glass down on the table with a clunk. "Why do I get the feeling that you're poking fun at me?"

She tossed the hat aside and bent over and shook her damp hair. "I've never been more serious."

The towel dropped to the floor, and she dug one foot beneath it and flipped it back into her arms. Then, methodically, she placed it around her shoulders, leaving everything else totally and completely exposed. But the way she was sitting cast sexy shadows over her most intimate parts, leaving only the sensual feminine shapes and curves tauntingly visible.

"Is that all you have to say?" she asked, pretending to be preoccupied with smoothing the towel.

"All?" he repeated, completely caught up in her towel tricks. "We've just started. I want you to understand where I stand. I can see us trying to make our relationship work, learning to live together, struggling to make ends meet, and your son moving in and saying, 'Mommy, I love you, and who's that man in your bed?"

She threw her head back and laughed. "You *have* had it pretty rough, Mac. And I sympathize with that part of your life. I really do. But none of that relates to me."

He shook his head and gestured with both hands in frustration. "That's because you aren't listening to me."

"I am! I know what you're saying. Did you finish your tale of '*real* adult problems'?"

He nodded sullenly.

"In my opinion, there is only one issue at stake here." She disengaged herself from the chair and walked toward him, holding both ends of the towel, which graced her shoulders like a shawl. She was totally exposed and completely vulnerable. "That one issue is..." She stopped before him. "Do you love me?"

Mac drew in a ragged breath as his gaze traveled up her body to her eyes. His voice was gravelly. "You know I do."

Tears filled Darlene's eyes. She could hardly believe her ears and yet, it was exactly what she wanted to hear. She was filled with the urge to shout for joy! "That's all I need to know." She reached out and took his hands and placed them on her waist. They felt large and warm and rough on her bare skin. Shivering with anticipation, she slid her hands up his arms and around his shoulders, then leaned forward and kissed him. She pressed her lips hard and demandingly on his—the way she wanted him tonight.

His reaction was immediate, and it encouraged her. She definitely felt in charge tonight. As she slid her tongue between his willing lips, she lowered herself onto his lap.

Even through his clothes, she could feel his body responding to hers. Darlene had heard what she came to hear. *He loved her.* And she was feeling with him what she wanted to feel. Oh, yes. She had him tonight—tonight and forever—and she'd never let go.

"I love you, too, Mac. Between us, we'll work it out. I promise."

His hands circled her waist, then moved to embrace her back and clasp her to him. He opened his thighs and tucked her into the vee of his body. His tongue sought hers, probing the source of her breathless kisses.

"Love me, Mac," she murmured between tiny kisses that she showered over his face. "Hold me. Show me you love me." She unbuttoned his shirt and, brushing her hands along his body, peppered kisses over his chest. Then she reached boldly between them to unzip his jeans.

They were grappling, reaching, struggling. Finally he muttered, "Let me—"

She switched off the lamp, then watched as he finished stripping off his clothes in the muted light. Soon he stood as naked as she in the firelight. The flames licked into the room's darkness, casting dancing shadows over their bodies. Broad shoulders connected with the thick expanse of his hair-covered chest. His strong arms waited to hold her. His erect manhood was ready to claim her.

Mac gazed at her like a man in a hypnotic spell. She was utterly beautiful, and he could hardly resist wrestling her to the floor this minute. Her breasts rose and fell. Her breathing grew faster. He wanted to touch, to devour, every part of her. But he waited for her, not touching, not kissing. Waited in agony.

Darlene could hear his labored breathing. She could feel his heated energy. She wanted him—probably as much as he obviously wanted her. As they stood there so close but not touching, every emotion she'd ever felt for Mac drew together to the center of her body in a knot of driving desire. She'd loved him, envied him, admired him, even hated him... and all of those explosive feelings welled inside her as they faced off. She'd never felt so tormented by one man. Nor so loved.

She placed her palms on his waist and gently pushed him toward the sofa. "Here," she demanded softly. "Now."

He fell backward onto the sofa, and she went with him. She stretched her body over his, kissing and enticing and inflaming him. She slithered and stroked her way from his earlobes to his navel to his groin, and all the areas in between, until he grabbed her and pressed her close.

"You're driving me crazy, Darlene . . . darlin'." His hands framed her hips and lifted.

They merged, writhing together in a frenzy of impatient sex. Sounds of delight mingled with the rainstorm outside as they sought their greatest satisfaction in each other.

It was a long, long time before either of them stirred. She snuggled on his chest, relishing the glow that had replaced the hard knot of desire inside her.

Mac stroked her back, content for the moment.

Darlene purred softly and placed occasional kisses on his chest. "Mac . . ."

"Hmm?"

"I love you so much."

"Hmm, the feeling's mutual."

"I love you so much I'd do most anything to keep you."

"Is that why you came over here tonight? To seduce me?"

"Yes." She laughed softly and caressed his thigh.

"Evil woman."

"It worked."

"I won't ever forget tonight. It was the best."

"Will you love me tonight and forever?"

"Of course."

As she lay in his arms, Darlene vowed to see that he kept his promise. Before they slept, she loved him again. And again at dawn.

A WEEK LATER, Darlene surveyed her squirming passengers. "Are we all ready? Everybody buckled?"

"Yes, ma'am," Emma and Byron chorused from the back seat.

"Ready as I'll ever be," Ida replied, snapping her seat belt with great effort. "Do I *have* to use this thing?"

"Yes!" Everyone responded in unison.

"Always use your seat belt, Gran. Because we care," Emma piped.

"No lectures from the peanut gallery," Ida scolded, glancing over her shoulder.

Both kids giggled.

"Okay, we're off!" Darlene started the motor of Ida's car and backed out of the driveway.

"I'm so excited," Emma said. "I've never been to an airport before. Will we get to see big jets?"

"Of course, stupid," Byron answered.

"Now, you two, don't get started," Ida warned.

"That's right," Darlene agreed. "I'll just let you stay here and clean the cabins with your dad if you're going to fight."

"We'll be quiet," Byron pledged with a glaring look at his sister. "I sure don't want to be left here and miss a trip to Knoxville."

"I've seen Ken's picture," Emma informed him. "I'll bet I recognize him first."

"No way!" Byron objected, and another argument ensued from the back seat.

Darlene glanced at Ida. "Thanks for coming with me to get Ken today. I'm so nervous."

"Are you sure you want us tagging along, girl?"

"Oh, yes! This will make it so much easier for both of us. It's been a long time since I've seen Ken. From my letters, he knows all about every one of you. You're my friends, and I want him to meet you. I think having the kids along is going to make it easier for us to mix."

"Darlene," Byron asked, "are we still going to stop for pizza on the way back home?"

"Only if there's no fighting on the way to the airport."

"All right!" they chorused again.

"Does your son know about Mac?" Ida asked softly.

"Oh, yes," Darlene responded confidently, then hedged. "Well, sort of. He knows Mac is a very good friend, and . . . I think he'll understand about Mac and me once he gets here."

"And what does Mac have to say about Ken coming here?"

Darlene turned onto the highway and accelerated before she answered. "Not much."

"He doesn't know, does he?"

"Well, he doesn't know Ken is coming right now."

"Darlene . . . you're springing this on him?"

"Not exactly. I did say that I'd like for him to meet Ken someday."

"And he said . . ."

Darlene shrugged. "Okay."

"Then why didn't you tell him Ken's coming now?"

"Take it easy, Ida. I know what I'm doing. It'll be all right. Trust me."

"And what *are* you doing?"

"Just a surprise, that's all."

Ida shook her head. "I don't know, Darlene. Sounds risky to me."

"Look. I almost lost Mac the last time I mentioned Ken. This time I want him to see for himself what a neat kid Ken is before he has a chance to reject him."

"I hope Mac doesn't feel deceived again. Especially since we were all in on this scheme of yours."

Darlene frowned and drove on in silence. With all her heart, she hoped her plan would work.

As they settled into the trip, Ida pulled out her hand sewing. She and Darlene discussed details and variations on the Britches-family idea, and which dolls to enter in the contest. Both of them had been working day and night on the new project. The deadline for entry was rapidly approaching and since Ken was coming, they knew Darlene would be spending her free time with him.

When they arrived at the airport, Darlene was a nervous wreck. She'd never had Ken come to visit her. It had always been the other way around, with her returning to their hometown. Darlene hoped Ken liked her friends, her new home, Mac, and . . . even her. Oh, Lord, she was having doubts about everything!

Emma clutched Darlene's hand and skipped along beside her in the long terminal corridor. "This is fun! I'm so glad you brought us, Darlene."

"Me, too." Darlene smiled at her. Having her friends around helped. She felt as if they were family and wanted Ken to like them as much as she did. Maybe she was expecting too much. Maybe he'd take one look and— No, she wouldn't let negative thoughts creep in at this stage.

"I bet he'll like Byron best because they're both boys," Emma said with a begrudging tone in her voice.

Darlene smiled at Emma sympathetically. "Well, they're closer in age, so you might expect that. But I think he'll like you, too."

"Yeah?"

"He doesn't have a sister, so he might think you're pretty neat—" she squeezed Emma's hand "—because you are."

"Why doesn't he have a sister?"

"Because I . . . don't have any other children."

"If he's your son, why doesn't he live with you?"

"Because I've never had a real home for him. So he stayed with my brother. Chase takes care of him, sort of like your grandma takes care of you." She paused to see if Emma understood.

"Is he coming to live with you?"

"No, honey. He's only visiting for a week."

"Does your brother want Ken to come here?"

"Why, he must. He paid for Ken's plane ticket." Darlene knew, though, that Chase did not want Ken to come live with her. They'd been through that many times.

"Wow! I wish I had an uncle like that."

"Ken's lucky. His uncle loves him very much."

"As much as you do?"

Darlene pressed her lips together. "Yes, I'm afraid he does." She led the way to the computer screen and showed the kids how to read the flight schedules. "This one's Ken's flight. And it's on time. Won't be long now!" They walked down the long corridor to the landing gate and waited at the proper spot.

Waiting had never been something Darlene did well. What she needed right now was a cigarette. She paced. If she had a cigarette, she'd have something to do, something to occupy her hands and her mouth. She sat down, then stood and paced some more. If Ida and the kids hadn't been with her, she'd have gone to that gift shop and bought a pack. No one would have known. Except Ken.

Quickly Darlene scrubbed that idea. She went to the window and stared at the planes landing and taking off, willing one of them to be Ken's. Finally it was there, rolling up to the gate. Darlene was perspiring as she watched each passenger. And she forgot about cigarettes. Ken dominated everything.

When the lanky, sandy-haired kid stepped through the doorway, Emma recognized him first and shrieked excitedly, "There he is! There's Ken!"

The boy looked startled and somewhat embarrassed at having his name called. He searched for a familiar face.

Darlene moved forward, thinking Ken looked bigger and older than ever. Where was her little boy?

With a crooked grin, he greeted her. "Hi, Mom."

"It's so good to see you, Ken!" Unable to hold back another minute, Darlene threw her arms around him and kissed his cheek. Then she pulled back. "Sorry about that. I don't want to embarrass you in front of all these people."

"It's okay," Ken conceded with a shy smile. "Suzanna warned me. She said everybody gets kissed in airports."

"Suzanna, huh?" Darlene felt a moment's jealousy that Suzanna had daily contact with her son and she didn't.

"But she didn't say someone would yell my name out in the airport! Who's the kid?"

"She's a friend of mine." Darlene hooked her arm in Ken's. "Come on. I brought several friends along for you to meet. We're going to have so much fun this week!"

Darlene introduced him to everyone. The two boys greeted each other quietly, both suddenly shy. But not Emma.

"He's bigger than I expected," she blurted.

"Me, too," Darlene admitted and glanced at her son with admiration. He'd grown since she'd last seen him and was almost as tall as she. She hadn't expected that. Her little boy was growing up, and it made her more determined than ever to include him in her life now. They'd been separated for too long.

As the group started for the baggage-claim area, Emma skipped alongside Ken. "Darlene promised we could stop for pizza on the way home. Are you hungry for pizza?"

"Heck, yeah! All they had on the plane was . . ."

Darlene smiled and released a contented sigh. So far, so good.

MAC WATCHED DANNY take a bucket of grain out to the deer and say goodbye. He'd be heading for college next week, and Mac had agreed to watch out for the animal. In a short while Danny returned, with the deer following close behind, like a puppy. Even though it was now free to roam, it returned to eat.

"You don't think this will be dangerous for him to be so comfortable with people, do you, Mac?"

"Well, it's not great, but there's no hunting in this part of the forest, so he's safe as long as he stays around here."

"Do you think he'll forget me while I'm gone?"

"Not for the few months you'll be away. Knoxville isn't that far. You'll be back before you know it."

Danny looked doubtful. "Thanksgiving's the first big break. That's months from now."

"You're not getting cold feet about leaving, are you, Danny?"

"Well, it *will* be different."

"Ah, once you get a taste of college life, you'll love it. We'll have to beg you to come back home for a visit."

"I know I'll miss home. But I'll especially miss you, Mac. Thanks for letting me keep my animals here. And for everything."

"I'll miss you coming around, too, Danny. But, you know something? It all paid off for me when you got that scholarship."

Danny grinned to hide his pride. "If it weren't for that, I might not be going to college. Especially not to the University of Tennessee."

"You'll do fine, Danny. And you'll make your daddy proud."

Danny looked up at Mac. "I'd rather make you proud, Mac. You've helped me so much."

"You've already made me proud, Danny. Real proud." Mac shook Danny's outstretched hand, then grabbed him in a rough, back-clapping, man-to-man hug.

After Danny had gone, Mac sat on the back porch and watched the deer nose around the yard. After a while, he seemed to lose interest with Danny not there.

Mac wandered into the house, feeling aimless and lost. He should be happy that Danny was heading off into such a promising future. But he would miss Danny. Normally, at a time like this, Mac would call Darlene. He needed a friend, and she was his best.

But today she wasn't home. She and Ida had taken the kids shopping for school in Knoxville.

He and Darlene still hadn't come to grips with the problem of her child. He knew very little about the kid. And, frankly, he didn't *want* to know. He saw Ken as the one major obstacle that could come between them. Darlene had a typical mother's obsession about the boy, and Mac knew it would cause problems. He'd been through that before. *He knew.*

And yet, he couldn't stay away from Darlene. He had tried. Even after that night when she'd come over to seduce him and he had succumbed so willingly, he'd tried to cool their relationship. But he couldn't push her out of his mind or his life.

He'd even gone over to her place twice this week and been content just to watch her sew her dolls. She and Ida had been busy trying to meet the deadline for entries into the Native Mountain Crafts Contest, so he'd had to wait until she had time for him. And he had waited, like a puppy, eager for any attention she might give him.

But when she did give him attention, she was wonderful. Mac thrived on it. One thing troubled him, though. She was working like crazy to enter that craft contest so she could win the prize money. It was more than enough to fly her back home to Arkansas. *To her son.*

They'd talked about the possibility of living together. But Darlene wasn't receptive to that idea. She wanted her independence or else a stronger commitment. He knew that she meant *marriage,* although neither had mentioned the word. They hadn't resolved the problem of bringing her son into their lives if they should marry.

Mac felt, however, that when Darlene achieved the financing she needed, she would go back to her family in Arkansas. Then what? Did she expect him to go with her? Or did she just plan to leave him?

If given the opportunity, what *would* she do?

He didn't want to think about the possibilities. How could he compete with her son? He wouldn't have a chance. But could he also place her in the position of choosing? That, too, was unfair.

He heard a noise on the front porch, then a brisk knock. It sounded like Darlene. He hurried to the door and swung it open.

"Hi, Mac." Flushed and slightly breathless, she stepped inside. "I'd like you to meet my son, Ken. Ken, this is my... friend, Mac."

Mac's heart leaped to his throat as he stared at the lanky, sandy-haired kid with big brown eyes like Darlene's.

10

DUMBFOUNDED, MAC STARED for a moment at the boy, then at Darlene. He tried to get a grip on his emotions. This kid who stood almost shoulder-to-shoulder with her was *her child.* They even had the same dark and devilish brown eyes. His sandy-colored hair was a little darker than hers. But he had the same spunky, proud expression on his youthful face. Maybe it was a family trademark.

The drama reminded him of a grade-B movie—*And Here Is Your Long-lost Son*... only this one was Darlene's. Mac had the impulse to laugh sarcastically, to yell his frustration. But this was too serious. And it was real.

He stroked his beard and forced a greeting. "Hi."

Ken boldly stuck his hand out for a shake. "Hi, Mac. Nice to meet ya at last."

"Yeah. You, too. Uh, come in. Come on in and have a seat." He stepped back, and the two surprise guests entered.

Darlene and Ken sat down side by side on the sofa. Mac sat in the chair. He crossed one ankle over his knee and cleared his throat. Tension fairly crackled in the air. He could tell this wouldn't be easy.

Ken was the first to speak. "Darlene, er...Mom says you're an expert fly fisherman."

"Well, I don't know about *expert,* but I have caught a few freshwater rainbow trout." Mac shrugged, trying to get a grip on his emotions as he faced the kid who called Darlene "Mom." "I take tourists fishing upstream and try to help them catch a trout while they're in the Smokies. Sometimes it works."

"We do the same thing at the Boon Docks, our fishing village in Arkansas," Ken said with childish eagerness to compare their life-styles. "Only there, tourists rent our boats and take themselves fishing. Mostly they go for large-mouth bass, but we have a few speckled trout. Last year we added houseboats to our fleet. They've been real popular with the renters."

In spite of himself, Mac warmed to Ken's friendliness. "I've heard that fishing's pretty good in the Bull Shoals area of Arkansas."

"It is. You should try it sometime. Dad would be glad to outfit you."

Mac pursed his lips together and nodded doubtfully. His eyes traveled to Darlene. "Uh-hmm."

"Ken has his own business at the Boon Docks," Darlene explained with a touch of pride and ignoring Mac's sarcasm. "Besides helping Chase with the boats and restaurant, that is."

"Oh?" Mac looked curiously at the boy. "What kind of business?"

"Aw, it's just a little worm farm that I've had since I was about eight." Ken gave his mother an embarrassed glance and shifted uncomfortably.

"But it's gotten bigger," Darlene encouraged. "It's more than a *little* worm farm now."

"I supply our fishing village and three other marinas," Ken admitted.

"Sounds like you're a pretty good entrepreneur if you have a business that's grown over the years," Mac commented. He had to hand it to the kid. He wasn't the average eleven-year-old.

"That's what Dad says. He says private business is the only way to go. The way I look at it is that the worms give me my spending money. Trouble is, now that my business has gotten so big it takes a lot of time."

"Who's taking care of this active business while you're here?" Mac asked.

"My partner." Ken grinned at Mac. "He's really my half brother. Sometimes he's a pain in the neck, but most times Ross is a pretty good kid. Dad married last year, and Suzanna has a son who's a couple of years younger than me. Ross just came with the territory."

Mac leaned back and studied Ken. Here was the touchy part—the extended-family-plus problems. "You two must get along okay if you've made him your business partner."

"Yeah. Most of the time." Ken shrugged. "You know how it is. Some things won't change, no matter how much you don't like them. So you might as well make the best of them."

Mac chewed his lip and pondered the down-to-earth philosophy of this kid. What did he know, anyway?

Darlene quickly picked up on Ken's discontent. "Don't you like Suzanna?"

"Yeah. She's okay. But she—"

"She isn't mean to you, is she?"

"Oh, no. It's not that. It's just that she takes up so much of Dad's time, we don't get to do all the things we used to do. Not alone, anyway. He wants to drag her everywhere we go." He made a face at Mac. "Dad and Suzanna are mush-ee!"

"They've only been married about a year," Darlene explained to Mac. Then, to Ken she said, "My main concern is that she's good to you."

"Oh, yeah. That's no problem." Ken shrugged and leaned forward. "She makes the best chocolate-chip cookies in the world!"

"Oh. That's good." Darlene squirmed. "Well, I make a pretty good chocolate-fudge cake. I'll make you one while you're here."

"Okay." Ken's attention changed from food to fishing. "Hey, Mac, Mom says you tie your own dry flies. And that you can keep a casting line doubled in the air for two minutes. I'd like to see that."

Mac laughed. "I see your mom's been talking a lot."

"I had to practice my typing somehow." Darlene responded as if that were the main purpose for writing to Ken. "Plus, I wanted Ken to know all about my friends here in Gatlinburg."

"It worked. I feel like I've known them all my life."

Mac gave Darlene a curious look with one raised eyebrow. *All about her friends?* Had she told her son everything about them? That they were lovers? That they had fought over the secret of his existence and over his possible intrusion into their lives?

"She also told me about the deer you have that follows you around like a pup," Ken added.

Mac launched into the story of how Danny had found the wounded deer and brought him here. And how, now that the young buck was all well and free, he kept coming around for food. "Would you like to see him?"

"Now? Sure thing!" Ken hopped up eagerly.

Mac, too, was glad to be active and not sitting in that miserable little face-to-face circle. He headed for the door, then paused and looked at Darlene. "Want to come along?"

She stood and shook her head. "No. You two go on and see if you can find the deer by yourselves. He probably won't come if there're too many strangers. I'll just, uh, make supper. Do you have any ground beef?"

"Sure. Why don't we fix hamburgers on the grill?"

"That'd be great," she said with a relieved smile. "I'll get everything ready. How about French fries?"

"Mom's gonna cook?" Ken teased, flashing a grin her way. "That'll be the day!"

"I'll show you," she claimed defiantly. "I make darn good fries!"

"How hard are fries to prepare?" Mac nudged Ken and the two walked away laughing.

Darlene let them have their laughter. She felt it was important for them to become friends. She hoped the deer would help draw them together, as well as their mutual interest in fishing. Pushing back the brown-and-white check curtains she had made for Mac, Darlene watched as Mac and Ken walked across the backyard together. Her heart pounded with a mixture of pride and anticipation. She wanted Ken to like Mac. And oh, God, how she wanted Mac to like Ken!

Mac pointed toward the woods. She could see him talking to Ken as they stood very still, searching the trees for the deer. Darlene couldn't help wondering what he was saying. More than that, however, she wondered what he was thinking.

Had he been offended by her walloping surprise? She had just wanted him to meet Ken and to see that a relationship could be developed if both of them worked at it.

Bless Ken. He'd even admitted how he gets along with his stepbrother by making the best of it. That attitude was something Chase had probably taught him. It sounded like her big brother. It wasn't bad advice, either.

She watched Mac draw closer to the line of trees, then halt. Ken followed stealthily and stopped, too. They were focused on something in the woods. Darlene held her breath as the regal, velvety brown head of Danny's deer appeared between the pines. Slowly, delicately, the animal picked its way toward Mac and the bucket of grain that he held to entice it. Ken looked as if he were spellbound. He'd probably never been close enough to a wild deer to touch it. That definitely would be something special to take back to Arkansas with him.

Darlene smiled. Maybe it hadn't been such a bad idea to bring Ken here, after all. She'd never doubted Ken's ability to like Mac; Ken had proven his adaptability many times. Her worry was that those feelings wouldn't be reciprocated by Mac.

By the time they returned, Darlene had the hamburgers on the grill and the fries cooking.

"Hey, Mom!" Ken called out excitedly as he rushed into the kitchen. "I had him eating out of my hand! He actually nibbled the grain from my palm! Gosh! What a feeling! All soft and sort of tickling. Wait'll Dad hears about this!"

Mac stood in the doorway as Darlene smiled at her son and slid her arm around his shoulders. He could see the touch of pain in her eyes when Ken mentioned the man he called "Dad." It must hurt to know that her own child felt such strong affection for her brother, not for her. In that brief moment, he saw that she *had* to do this. She had to develop a relationship with Ken before time slipped away and she lost him completely. Mac realized that she would allow nothing—or no one—to block her way. And he knew that, unfortunately, he stood completely outside the tight mother-and-son unit.

After supper, Mac nudged Ken's arm. "I'd say your mom did okay on those hamburgers and fries, wouldn't you?"

"Yeah! Much better than McDonald's," Ken agreed.

"So why don't we fix dessert?"

"We? Like, you and me?" Ken looked doubtfully at Mac. "Like, what do you suggest?"

"Like, cherry pie," Mac replied with a grin. "Do you like it?"

"Sure, but I can't make a pie."

"I'll show you."

Darlene narrowed her eyes at Mac. "You catch fish and make pies, too? This I want to see."

"Multitalented," Mac quipped, flashing a smile her way.

"I want to see you tie those flies," Ken added.

"Pie, first." Mac opened the cabinet and pulled out several items. "Then I'll show you my rig where I work on the flies."

"I don't want to just see them. I want to learn how to make them," Ken said frankly.

"Okay, then. We'll tackle that tomorrow. Do you want to help me with this pie, or don't you want to eat any of it?" Mac set out a pan and a big bowl.

"Yes, sir," Ken answered quickly with a grin. "I want to learn to make pie first. I *really* want to learn that."

"All right. Open that can. Then pour it in here. . . ."

Darlene chuckled and shook her head as the two poured, measured, stirred, and managed to get flour and cherry juice all over the cabinet, the floor, and each other.

When they finally popped the less-than-skillful culinary creation into the oven, Mac folded his arms and smiled at Darlene. "So, there. A pie in thirty minutes."

"I'm impressed," Darlene responded, motioning with her thumb to the oven. "You two really did a number on the pie. And, on the kitchen."

"Aw shucks," Mac said with a thicker-than-usual accent. "'Tweren't nothin'."

"Well, since you guys worked so hard to make the pie, I'll clean up the kitchen," Darlene offered. She started running hot water into the sink and generously poured in some detergent. "The real proof," she couldn't help adding, "is in the eating."

"You're going to love it," Mac promised. "I'll help clean up our mess. Ken, why don't you go into the living room and play some music? There are plenty of cassettes on that shelf above the stereo."

"Okay!" Ken hustled to the other room, eager to get out of cleanup detail.

"Thanks, Mac," Darlene told him when the stereo was blasting with Oingo Boingo.

"It's just an easy throw-together cobbler that Ida taught me to make for those times when a pie wasn't possible."

"I'm talking about the way you're treating Ken," she murmured seriously. "I appreciate it more than you know."

"Didn't you know how I'd treat him, Darlene? Don't you trust me?"

"Oh, Mac, I knew you two would get along. Of course, I trust you!"

"Then why didn't you tell me you were bringing him?"

"I...I'm sorry. I realize it was a big surprise. But I—"

"Aren't we friends and lovers in every sense?"

"Yes, and...I guess I wanted you to see him and get to know him before you made a judgement about him, Mac. I don't think he'll come between us, do you?"

Mac stuffed his hands into his jeans pockets. "Ken's a great kid. He's fun and mature for a kid his age, but—"

"But what?"

"But I can't tell you what he'll do or how he'll react toward us. I saw a kid change right before my eyes!"

"Look, Ken's mature because he's always lived with adults and has had to grow up quickly. In some ways, he's had it pretty rough, I guess. He has a family with Chase, but I want to still be his mom."

"I can see that."

"Can you blame me?"

Mac looked away for a second. "No."

Darlene gave Mac a quick kiss.

Later, when the evening wound down and the pie plate was licked clean, Darlene reluctantly announced, "We've got to go home, Ken."

"Yeah, I have an early tour tomorrow," Mac said.

"A fishing tour? Could I go along?" Ken asked eagerly. "I've always wanted to learn fly-casting. Dad is always too busy to teach me."

"If it's okay with your mom."

"You sure, Mac?" Darlene gathered their plates and headed for the kitchen. "He won't be in the way of your paying clients?"

"Course, I'm sure. I'd love to have him along." He looked at Ken. "Be ready at oh-five-hundred."

"Huh?"

"That's the military way of saying five o'clock."

Without batting an eyelash, Ken nodded. "Okay. Sure. But I don't have any equipment."

"I'll take care of it." Mac grabbed his Jeep keys from the desk, then halted. "Doesn't it make more sense if you spend the night here? Then we can get ready together and not disturb anyone, like your mother."

"Yeah." Ken turned to Darlene. "Can I, Mom?"

She blinked. Truthfully, she wanted to stay, too. But, of course, she couldn't. "If it's all right with Mac."

"It was my suggestion."

"Well, okay." She could think of no good reason for him not to stay, except the irony of the whole thing.

"I'll take you home." Mac steered her to the door, then added for Ken, "Go ahead and take a shower. You can use the bedroom down the hall and to the left. I'll be right back."

When they were alone in the Jeep, she said. "This is so weird. Isn't that the same room you gave me a few months ago? Now you're putting my son up for the night."

Mac started the motor. "A few months ago, I would never believe you could have a son that big. Or that nice."

"He *is* pretty neat, isn't he?" Darlene smiled proudly.

"He's great. Your brother must be some terrific person."

"Yep." She nodded and sighed. "He's great, too. Just like his kid."

"No. Ken's *your* kid, Darlene. Don't ever lose sight of that."

"I don't intend to," she said quietly. "But Chase has done most of the raising, and I recognize what a good job he's done."

"But you're not finished with him, are you?"

Darlene lifted her chin and gazed with her old defiance at Mac. "Not by a long shot."

KEN STAYED IN GATLINBURG for six days. Darlene was amazed at how easily she adapted to having him around—and at how fast the time went. He helped her get her work done each day, and then they played. They hiked in the woods and followed the mountain streams.

And they talked, getting a chance to know each other for the first time.

Mac taught Ken to fly-cast and how to make a few simple dry flies for catching mountain trout. And the two of them fished almost daily.

At night, they would go to the Blevinses for card games or Monopoly and Ida's homemade cookies. Some evenings, Mac would join them. For Darlene, it was a heavenly time. She had her son and dearest friends close. It was the longest stretch she'd ever spent with Ken. Better yet, she had him almost to herself, with no interference from her brother, Chase.

The night before Ken was to leave, they all had a grand party for him. Mac fried trout and Darlene made hush puppies. Ida fixed slaw and a huge chocolate cake. Boyd cranked the ice-cream maker for homemade peach ice cream. They played backyard softball and at dark, the boys played hide-and-seek with Emma, taking turns jumping out and scaring her. Finally they made peace by catching her a jarful of lightning bugs.

"More ice cream, Mac?" Darlene scooted next to him on the bench.

"No, thanks. I'm stuffed." His arm automatically went around her shoulders, and they watched the kids playing for a few minutes. "This has been a terrific evening. Great food."

She nestled against him and sighed. "Yeah. I hate to see it end."

"He'll have some nice memories to take back to Arkansas."

"I wish he didn't have to go back," Darlene admitted.

"Yeah. I can tell." He shifted and looked down at her. "Look, I wasn't invited, but I'd like to take you and Ken to Knoxville to the airport tomorrow."

She smiled gratefully. "Would you, Mac? Do you have time?"

"Of course. I'll make time."

"Good. I'd like that." She settled against his shoulder and tried not to think of what it would be like when Ken left and things were quiet again.

THE NEXT DAY WAS sunny and crisp—a beautiful Smoky Mountain day. But Darlene didn't notice. She just dreaded the thought of saying goodbye to Ken.

By the time Mac arrived, Darlene had plastered a smile on her face. He was a little surprised by her upbeat attitude. She *was* gutsy. She'd lived most of her life wearing a carefree facade, and she put it on today for her son. They talked and teased all the way to the airport.

At the gate Darlene walked to the window with Ken. She put her hand on his shoulder, and for a few minutes they silently watched the planes land and take off.

Finally she said, "I've had a wonderful time, Ken. Hope you have, too."

"Yeah. This was great. Our best ever!"

She laughed, remembering some of their awkward visits. "I think so, too. I wish you could stay with me."

"Well, I've got school and all...."

"I know. But will you come visit me again sometime?"

"Sure. Anytime."

"You will?" Darlene looked surprised.

He shrugged. "Just let me know."

"Oh, Ken, I'd love that," Darlene said eagerly. "I want you to come back again, real soon. Maybe for the holidays. You know . . . I love you, Ken. I've missed not having you around."

"I love you, too, Mom."

She hugged him tightly, then kissed him. Never had their bond been closer, never had he responded quite so positively to her. Yes, things were changing. And for the better. They had a pretty good relationship, after all. And it would improve if they worked at it. She was filled with pride and love—filled to overflowing.

Ken hugged her back, but when the kissing started, he squirmed. "Okay-okay! Enough of the mushy stuff, Mom. I think I'm supposed to board soon."

Darlene and Mac watched the jet taxi down the runway and take off, circling around to head westward. Neither of them said a word for a long time. Mac placed his arm around her. He could feel the tension in her shoulders and see the pain in Darlene's downturned face as she bravely stood beside him. It hurt him to the core to see her like that. "You know, Darlene, you don't have to pretend with me."

It was all the encouragement she needed. She turned her face against him and cried.

Even as he held her, Mac couldn't shake the feeling that for two cents, Darlene would be on that plane with Ken, flying back where she belonged.

With her son.

How could he deny her those natural feelings of a mother for her child? He couldn't.

That night, Darlene stayed over with Mac. It was the first time they had been alone together all week.

She pressed her slim naked body close to his. "Thanks for going with me today, Mac. It helped to have you there."

He wrapped his big arms around her and held her with all the tenderness he could muster. He knew she was hurting and felt absolutely helpless to ease her pain. "I was glad to go along, Darlene. He's a good kid, and I...like him."

"You do?" Her voice was small in the darkness.

"Of course. He's a neat kid."

"Credit Chase for most of that."

"What about genes? His mother's a pretty neat lady."

"Who dropped out of school and has accomplished nothing in her life," she muttered with a sigh.

"That's not true, Darlene, and you know it."

"I'd just like to make him proud of me."

"Don't you think he's proud of you now?"

"No reason for him to be." She thought for a minute. "He did say he was glad I'd dumped Wiley."

"Me, too."

She kissed his chest. "I guess I've done *something* good for me. Like being around you, Mac."

He stroked her back. "You're terrific, Darlene. And I love you."

She cherished his admission, spoken so softly in the dark of night. Just as she cherished Mac—more every day.

DARLENE AND IDA had been busy all month preparing their entry in the Native Mountain Crafts Contest—

The Britches Family. Hours of designing had gone into creating each family member.

On the evening before the fair was to open, the winners of all the competitions would be announced. When Mac arrived to pick Darlene up, she was a wreck.

"You don't mind stopping for Ida, do you, Mac? I told her she could ride with us. Boyd's going to take my calls this evening. Only two of the cabins are rented, so there shouldn't be much. Did I put on my lipstick?" She smoothed her sweater and started for the bathroom. "Let me check—"

"Hold on." Mac swept her against him and kissed her quickly. He touched his hands to her hair. "What did you do to your hair? It's different."

"Ida trimmed it for me. Looks better, don't you think?"

"Yes, I do. I think you look great." He kissed her again. "Calm down, honey. I don't know when I've ever seen you so nervous."

"But, Mac, it's *so* important!"

"You'll do well. Your dolls are beautiful. Almost as beautiful as you."

She smiled gratefully. "You're sweet. But you're also prejudiced. I don't know how dolls—*mere dolls*—will stack up against a quilt or wood carving or handmade musical instrument. There'll be so many good native mountain crafts."

"All I know is that you had a terrific idea. And you and Ida worked very hard to make those dolls good. And they *are* very good, no matter whether you win or not."

"I need that winning money so badly," she said, biting wistfully on her lower lip.

He held his breath. "What'll you do with the money if you win?"

"Why, it'll be enough for me to put my life back in order." Darlene gazed up at him with absolute clarity and assurance. This would provide the solution she'd needed for so long. It would buy her ticket home and sustain her until she could get another job in Arkansas.

Mac's blue eyes clouded. He felt as if someone had belted him in the stomach. She slipped from his embrace and quickly ran a brush through her hair before agreeing that she was ready to go.

The field house was crowded. Overwhelmed with curiosity and a nervousness that wouldn't allow them to sit still, Ida and Darlene inspected the competitive crafts on display. Mac lapsed into a worried silence as he sat at the back of the room, arms folded across his chest, and watched. He'd never felt so torn, so almost desperate to hold on to someone.

He wanted Darlene to win. She deserved it. Her creations were excellent. She needed this win to validate what she'd been doing these past few months.

But still, he feared her achievement. If she won, she'd use the prize money to return to her family—and leave him. Oh, God, he didn't want to lose her. And yet, it was inevitable—if not now, then soon.

A hush came over the crowd as members of the judging committee filed to the front of the room. Everybody took seats and listened anxiously for their names. Winners in every category, from buttermilk biscuits to silk-screen T-shirts, were announced. Then came the highly coveted Native Mountain Crafts Award.

Darlene's heart was pounding so loudly that she could barely hear the announcer briefly outlining the criteria for the award.

"We were looking for something that characterizes the mountain people for what they are and what they do. We see great potential in this winner. The artist has captured an ages-old craft and with unique creativity, brought it into contemporary society. The winning entry is The Britches Family of dolls, by Darlene Clements!"

With an ecstatic little yelp, Darlene bounded out of her seat. She hugged Mac and Ida, then rushed forward for her prize and numerous congratulations from everyone. Mac watched with a tight expression on his face. He wanted to be glad for her. But as he gazed at her happy face, he knew *this was it*.

Later, after he'd dropped Ida off, Mac drove to Darlene's cabin. He stopped the Jeep and sat there quietly for a moment. "Well, Darlene, you've done it. You accomplished what you set out to do. Congratulations, darlin'. I'm proud of you." He kissed her, hard and long.

When they finally pulled apart, she smiled up at him, unable to contain her happiness. "I've never won anything in my life."

"This wasn't a lucky win, Darlene. This was a reward for a brilliant, creative idea and hours of hard work. It's something you deserve."

"Thanks, Mac. I've never been rewarded so nicely for any work I've ever done. It's a good feeling."

"I'm sure Ken will be proud of you now."

"Think so?" She giggled delightedly.

"I know so. All of your family will be happy about this."

"I can't wait to call them." She opened the door, then noticed that Mac had made no effort to move. She clutched his hand. "Want to come in?"

Mac drew back and tried to sound nonchalant. "Not tonight. I have an early tour tomorrow."

"That never stopped you before," she said in a sexy, teasing tone.

He leaned back stiffly in the seat. "Not this time, Darlene. We may as well start getting realistic about this."

"What do you mean?"

"If you're going back to Arkansas as you said you would do with the prize money, we'll have to break this off. I just don't want to prolong it."

"You sound as if you can't wait to get rid of me."

"I'm not the one leaving."

"I haven't decided what I'm going to do with the prize money."

"I thought it was a foregone conclusion."

"Nothing is foregone, except maybe *us*." Stunned, by Mac's blunt comments and her own acid responses, Darlene stumbled up the porch steps and into her little cabin. It was the first time she'd come to grips with what it would mean to lose Mac. Even her phone call to Ken and the joyous congratulations from Chase and Suzanna couldn't cheer her. They all wanted to know when she'd be coming, but she couldn't answer. She'd let them know. Only Suzanna, her sister-in-law, perceived something amiss when she asked, "What about Mac? Will he be coming with you?"

Darlene knew it was a logical question. She'd always brought Wiley with her in the past. "I don't know," she admitted honestly. But in her heart, she knew that Mac didn't feel a part of her Arkansas family, and he wouldn't uproot his life at this point. The last thing in the world he probably wanted was to encourage her relationship with Ken.

That night, Darlene lay in bed alone, thinking what it would be like to always be without Mac. How would she manage without his encouragement, his wonderful strength, his everlasting love?

How in the world would she live without Mac? She hated the thought. And yet . . . there was no other way.

DARLENE SLEPT very little that night. She muddled through the day as a battle raged within her heart. How could she go after her son and still keep Mac? As the day wore on, the winner's award seemed more of a nemesis than a prize. Without it, there'd be no choices right now. But she knew, also, that without it, there'd be no opportunity.

When a stranger knocked at her door in midafternoon, she assumed it was the cabin guests she was expecting from Ohio. Instead, she greeted a woman who was alone and dressed to the teeth. Darlene was surprised at her appearance, for people usually arrived already in jeans and T-shirts, ready for a casual weekend in the mountains. "I'm looking for Darlene Clements."

Darlene peered through the screen door. She didn't recognize the woman and wondered how this stranger knew her name. "Well, you found her. I'm Darlene."

"Are you the creator of The Britches Family?"

"Along with my partner, Ida Blevins."

"Well, I've just come from the fair, and I'm very impressed with your winning creations, Darlene."

"Thanks . . . I think."

"I love The Britches Family. And I'd like to buy them. Uh, could I come in so we can talk?"

"Sure." Darlene held the door open for her fashionable guest. She was impressed and delighted that someone wanted to buy her dolls. This was only the first day of the fair, too.

"Excuse me. I'm Jaclyn Reich," the woman was saying as she glided into Darlene's tiny two-room cabin. "And I own a shop in New York. Have you ever heard of Greenwich Village?"

"Yes. Please have a seat." Darlene motioned to her single chair. She perched on the end of her bed and folded one jeaned-clad leg beneath her.

When Jaclyn sat, her long floral skirt draped to the floor. "I specialize in folk art, and I travel around the country to find the best and most marketable. That's what I consider your Britches Family, and I want to make you an offer you can't refuse. . . ."

IT WAS THREE business-filled days before Darlene had a chance to see Mac. He was sitting at the table on his back porch, tying flies, when she approached. "I figured you'd be around to tell me when you were leaving," he said without looking up at her. "So I've made a couple of special dry flies that I'd like you to take to Ken. I think they'll work for lake fishing, too."

"I'm too busy right now. I'm afraid you'll have to send them to him yourself," she retorted sassily.

"Now that you have the money, I figured you'd be leaving soon."

"Actually, I'm too busy to make the trip now. I'll probably wait until Thanksgiving."

Mac raised one eyebrow and looked at her. "Oh? Too busy doing what?"

"Getting my new business started."

He frowned. "What new business?"

"The business Ida and I are starting." Darlene looked sideways at him and ambled around the porch.

"Okay, Darlene. I'll bite. What are you up to now?"

She smiled impishly and launched into a description of her unusual visit from Jaclyn Reich. "And she wants to sell our dolls exclusively in her Greenwich Village shop. She's paying us a nice little sum for that privilege. I think she called it 'exclusivity.' Anyway, we have a contract and everything. I brought it along so you could take a look at it before I sign. *If* you don't mind."

Mac stopped what he was doing and gazed levelly at her. "Be happy to."

"So," Darlene continued, "Ida and I have to get busy. We've got so much work to do. We're going to start out hiring her friend, Mary Beth, in Knoxville. Fortunately she already has the basics of doll making. We're going to Knoxville later in the week to give her specific instructions for making our particular dolls and to deliver supplies. After that, most of her work will be conducted by mail."

"But when are you going to move—"

"To Arkansas?"

He nodded tightly.

"I'm not." Darlene folded her arms and leaned on the porch rail. "I'm staying right here."

Mac stormed to his feet. "But, what about your son? What about Ken, the kid who needs you?"

"Oh, I'll always be here for him. He knows that now. We've talked about this on the phone several times. He knows how I feel about him, how much I love him. But Ken has always lived with Chase. He loves it there. It's his home."

"Yours, too."

"Not really. I've been gone so long it doesn't feel right anymore." She shrugged and continued, "Anyway, Chase loves Ken very much, like a father. And the feeling's mutual. Plus, I promised him a long time ago that I wouldn't destroy that special relationship. Chase has Ken all set up in the family business. That's important to him."

Mac stood in front of her, his hands loosely hooked on his hips. "Let me see if I've got this straight. Then you aren't going to—"

"Take over as Ken's parent? Not at this late stage. The best I can do is retain a part-time relationship, have him visit me for holidays and summers. Of course, I'll try to fly over and see him on special occasions. Chase agreed to it. So did Ken. It's best for him."

Mac nodded silently. He couldn't believe what he was hearing.

"Anyway," she went on, "I can't give up everything I've got going here. I have to complete my high-school education. Ken'll never respect me if I don't do that. Driving into town for those refresher classes twice a week wasn't fun. I'd hate to stop now, when the GED test is so close. And after that, I may decide to go to college. Who knows?"

Mac stared at her, his blue eyes intense. He didn't know what to think. There were too many variables here that she'd never explained. Like her brother, Chase. And the exact role he played in Ken's life. And where she saw herself fitting into Ken's life at this point. And what the heck she was doing with her winnings.

"But I thought you were going to take the money and—"

"Run?" Darlene laughed. "Well, I considered it, believe me. But I realized that half the money really belongs to Ida. She helped me so much with this doll project that I have to include her. What can you do with five hundred?" She shrugged. "Not much. And now, we have this business deal with Jaclyn."

Mac thought he'd explode. "Darlene—"

"But then," Darlene continued as if she weren't itching to wrap her arms around him, "the worst of it is that I love you, Mac. Leaving would mean giving up the best love I've ever had. And I couldn't do that."

Mac coiled his arms around her. "I can't believe I'm hearing this right. Darlene, my darlin' Darlene, what would I do without you?"

She turned her face up to him. "You don't have to worry about that. You have to decide what to do *with* me now that you have me. I'm through rambling around the country. I'm ready to settle down, right here in Gatlinburg." She smiled faintly. "With you, if you'll have me."

He wedged her into the vee of his legs and held her close to his muscular frame. "That's no problem at all. I'm going to love you . . . forever." He lowered his face for a sweet and tender, long-lasting kiss.

When she finally lifted her lips from his, she said seriously, "Only one requirement. You must accept my son."

"Darlene, I was wrong to prejudge our situation. I love you more than I ever believed possible. You are the bright spot in my life. I respect your relationship with your son. Now that I've met him, I promise you that we'll get along just fine."

She kissed him fervently. "Oh, Mac, you're the best man I've ever known. I love you so much."

He returned the kiss. "You're the best thing that's ever happened to me, Darlene. I love you. . . ." His words dissolved into another kiss. "Looks like we might be making a trip to Arkansas for our honeymoon. Then maybe next summer, Ken could come and stay with us."

"Honeymoon?" she gasped. "You mean, *get married?*"

"That *usually* comes first. You *do* want me to meet the family, don't you?"

"Oh, Mac! *Marriage?*" Darlene couldn't believe her ears. Marriage was a dream for others. Never for her. Now Mac was talking love and marriage and a honeymoon, all in one breath.

"You're an amazing person, Darlene. When you're loved by the best, what other choice do we have but to make it together?" He kissed her again and lifted her into his arms and carried her inside . . . to love forever.

Epilogue

"ARE YOU SURE you want a baby hippo in your wedding party, Darlene?"

"Definitely!" Darlene laughed affectionately. She helped her sister-in-law adjust the sash of her stylish, dropped-waist maternity dress. "Here's your chance to show off a little. Lord knows, Chase is proud as a peacock of this." She patted Suzanna's stomach lightly. "You'd think no one else ever produced a baby before."

"Isn't he ridiculous?" Suzanna sighed, but Darlene could see the delight—or was it simply love?—in her violet eyes.

"Well, it's really Chase's first. Even though he's had Ken all these years, and now your son, Ross, this is your very own love-child."

"We've never thought of it that way, because Ken and Ross are our family. This is just another addition." Suzanna touched Darlene's hand. "We want you to know that our love for Ken won't be any different after the baby or after your marriage, Darlene."

"I understand. Chase and I talked about it. He thinks that Mac and I need a little adjustment time, you know. And I agree. Ken should stay in school here in Arkansas, where he's always lived. But he can visit us in Tennessee any time he wants to."

"And Mac... How does he feel?"

"He's looking forward to Ken's next visit." She propped her hands on her hips. "Do you know that he's making Ken a special short casting rod, just his size?"

"I'm not surprised. They did spend all of yesterday fishing while the rest of us were busy getting ready for the wedding."

"But that was important time together."

"Yep. Extremely." Suzanna paused then. "Do you know that Ken is very proud of you?"

Darlene looked up quickly. "Really?"

"Absolutely! He can't stop talking about the things his mom has done in Tennessee—especially the fact that your dolls are in a shop in New York City. Plus, he says that you've quit smoking. Is that true?"

Darlene nodded proudly. "I have no disgusting habits now. Isn't *that* disgusting?"

They both laughed.

"Hmm... What the love of a good man won't do." Suzanna smiled warmly. "And I thought you should know that Ken likes Mac very much."

"That's great to hear. Mac has a special way with kids. He just didn't realize that the trouble with his first marriage was with his former wife, not her son."

"You seem to be very happy. You even look different, Darlene. Sort of radiant."

Darlene beamed. "This is the happiest I've ever been, Suzanna. Mac is so wonderful. I'm very lucky to have found him."

"We happen to think he's pretty lucky, too." Suzanna hugged Darlene. "It's almost time. You know that Chase wants only the best for you, Darlene."

Darlene smiled happily. "Well, if my smart-aleck brother wants the best for me, he'll be completely satisfied. Because Mac is the finest man I've ever known. He's truly the best."

The door opened and Ellie Schafer, Suzanna's mother, poked her head in. "Are you girls ready? The fellows are getting antsy, especially the groom. Let's get on with this wedding!"

"Okay, Mama. We're ready," Suzanna said. She turned to Darlene and squeezed her hand. "Let's get you married to the best."

"I'll be right there." Darlene paused to glance out the tiny window that gave her a view of the river where she and Chase had grown up. All the poverty and misery and ugliness of their former life was gone. In its place now were new lives filled with families and happiness and love.

Today, after the ceremony, there would be a reception for the newlyweds. Darlene would be surrounded by the people who meant most to her—her son, her brother and his wife, and her new husband, Mac. And after their honeymoon, they would return to Gatlinburg to make their home near the most loving friends anyone could have. She'd never been happier.

She stepped out of the rest room into the gaily decorated restaurant and took her handsome brother's arm.

Chase kissed her cheek and squeezed her hand. "Ready for the plunge?"

She nodded confidently. "Let's do it."

As the wedding music swelled, they walked toward the small wedding party gathered by the floor-to-ceiling windows that overlooked Shoal Creek, Arkansas. No longer could Darlene and Chase be called "river rats"—that old nickname from years ago. They had shed that stigma and found beautiful, everlasting love.

Darlene glanced proudly over the group. Suzanna waited to serve as her matron of honor, and Ken stood beside Mac as his best man. She winked at her son. Then her gaze met Mac's, and she choked. Tears filled her eyes. There was no doubt in her mind that she was marrying the best man of all.